THE
MEXICAN

THE
MEXICAN

A novel by
Robert Westbrook

Based on the screenplay by
J.H. Wyman

A Gore Verbinski Film

DreamWorks

ONYX
Published by New American Library, a division of
Penguin Putnam Inc., 375 Hudson Street,
New York, New York 10014, U.S.A.
Penguin Books Ltd, 27 Wrights Lane,
London W8 5TZ, England
Penguin Books Australia Ltd, Ringwood,
Victoria, Australia
Penguin Books Canada Ltd, 10 Alcorn Avenue,
Toronto, Ontario, Canada M4V 3B2
Penguin Books (N.Z.) Ltd, 182–190 Wairau Road,
Auckland 10, New Zealand

Penguin Books Ltd, Registered Offices:
Harmondsworth, Middlesex, England

Published by Onyx, an imprint of New American Library,
a division of Penguin Putnam Inc.

First Printing, February 2001
10 9 8 7 6 5 4 3 2 1

TM & Copyright © DreamWorks, 2001
Interior photographs by Merrick Morton.
All rights reserved

 REGISTERED TRADEMARK—MARCA REGISTRADA

Printed in the United States of America

PUBLISHER'S NOTE
This is a work of fiction. Names, characters, places, and incidents either are
the product of the author's imagination or are used fictitiously, and any resem-
blance to actual persons, living or dead, business establishments, events, or
locales is entirely coincidental.

BOOKS ARE AVAILABLE AT QUANTITY DISCOUNTS WHEN USED TO PROMOTE
PRODUCTS OR SERVICES. FOR INFORMATION PLEASE WRITE TO PREMIUM MAR-
KETING DIVISION, PENGUIN PUTNAM INC., 375 HUDSON STREET, NEW YORK, NEW
YORK 10014.

One

The traffic signal goes through its lighted sequence: green . . . yellow . . . red. Over and over again, forever, as the throaty sounds of cars moving along Ventura Boulevard rise, then recede.

The signal light continues to strobe through the colors, until it finally settles on green, then flickers from green to red, oddly missing amber as the acrid smell of burning rubber and the screeching sound of twisting metal and crashing glass seem to fill Jerry's ears. . . .

Jerry Welbach woke from the recurring dream he'd been having maybe twice a week for the last five years. Rubbing his bleary, bloodshot eyes, he sighed aloud. Yet another nearly sleepless night plagued by the same nightmare.

Jerry swung his legs out of bed and sat on the

edge of the mattress; then he looked out the window to see the pale fingers of dawn creeping across the horizon. His head hammered, his heart still thumped rapidly, and his mouth was bone-dry.

He was in his early thirties, but mornings like these seemed to make him feel older than a fossil. His eyes were red and swollen from fatigue. A movement next to him in bed made him turn to look at Samantha. She had stirred slightly in her sleep and her face was very peaceful, like an angel's. She was beautiful at times like these, when she was quiet and asleep and not ragging at him: her reddish-brown hair spilled across the pillow, her naked shoulders poked up from the sheets.

As Jerry sat watching her, her eyes suddenly flickered open. Her head turned slightly toward the alarm clock on the nightstand. It read 6:59. A broad grin stretched across Sam's face as she saw that she had beaten the alarm by a full minute. As the radio clicked on, Sam turned to see Jerry watching her, and her grin broke into a dazzling smile. Jerry couldn't help but return her affectionate smile. It was a special day today, they both knew—one full of new possibilities and opportunities because they were finally able to get out of town for a well-deserved vacation.

As Sam closed her eyes again and snuggled back down into the comfort of the pillows, concern once again crept across Jerry's face. After all, they seemed to have it all right now. But Sam still wasn't happy, and she wanted to get out of town, which is why they had planned a little trip to Las Vegas to feel out the town and see if it would be worth a move. Sam had always talked of Vegas with great reverence, but Jerry wasn't as sure—after all, they had it all in L.A., so why throw caution to the wind? Especially right now, when Jerry had so many things he needed to take care of, things that he hadn't quite had the nerve to tell Sam about just yet.

They had a nice apartment in the Valley. You'd think she'd be happy here, but she wasn't. It baffled him that she wanted to move to Vegas—it truly did. And it made matters just a little dicey right now. The last thing Jerry needed right now was to screw things up with Sam.

Sometimes it seemed to Jerry Welbach that the entire world was on his case and wouldn't leave him alone. Right now, for instance the doorbell was buzzing repeatedly downstairs, with the annoying persistence of an alarm clock. Jerry continued to dress at his own speed, refusing to be rushed—a small rebellion but one that gave him some satisfaction. At last, he walked downstairs and opened the locks on the front door. Ted Shurker was standing on the hallway landing outside with a big grin on his face, radiating a whole lot of wattage this morning for a fifty-year-old gangster. Jerry felt exhausted just looking at him.

"You know I've been out here for fifteen minutes?" Ted mentioned, his smile taking on a knife-like edge.

"I thought you were in traffic," Jerry lied.

"I thought you were running late," Ted said, shrugging. He nodded meaningfully. "You got the paperwork?"

Jerry touched the documents that were in the inside pocket of his jacket.

Ted was relieved. "You're not pissed at me, are you?" he asked. "I mean, I'm just doing my portion here. You're my guy, Jerry."

Jerry nodded without enthusiasm.

"You're my guy, Ted."

Jerry grabbed his keys and stepped outside, closing the apartment door behind him. Together, they headed toward Ted's car.

Two

Margolese Holdings, Inc., was headquartered in a warehouse across town, in an industrial section of L.A. where people didn't walk at night, not unless they were armed to the teeth and had a few friends along.

Ted and Jerry passed through the huge bay doors into the vast interior of the warehouse. The noise here was deafening and harsh. They made their way past a forklift that was moving a pallet of PVC pipe, and up a flight of interior stairs to the illuminated second-floor offices above. At the top of the stairs they passed through a glass door into a lushly carpeted reception area. The office made an effort to look upscale and respectable. There were a few potted plants, vaguely modern paintings on the walls, and an expensive-looking sofa and several matching armchairs. But you could still hear the din from the warehouse below, and the furniture looked rented and generic, like it might be repossessed at any moment. As they entered the reception room, Bernie Nayman stepped out to greet them.

Nayman was a middle-aged man with a sour face, thin and neat, dressed conservatively in a dark business suit. He was the head accountant for Margolese Holdings, Inc., a man who did magic things with numbers.

"You get that fucking passport?" Nayman asked.

Jerry showed his passport, pulling it from his jacket pocket. Nayman nodded and unceremoniously pointed Jerry and Ted into his office. Jerry was starting to get an anxious feeling about all this. Nayman's office was full of polished wood and leather chairs, very posh, like an English club. Nayman's assistant, Bobby Victory, was lounging in one of the leather chairs, his legs comfortably crossed. He was younger than Nayman, in his thirties, with short-cropped blond hair that made him look more like a punk than an assistant accountant. Bobby stood up and positioned himself beside Nayman as he settled himself into his desk chair.

Nayman and Bobby were quite the team. Jerry stood with his stomach rumbling, wishing he wasn't here. He sighed and tried to explain.

"I've been sort've having a rough go of things lately, some problems with my life. Some personal things. My girlfriend, she's really . . . It's just, she doesn't seem to have the patience with me that she used to. We're fighting a lot and I'm a little distracted by it, if you want to know the truth. We go to a group . . ."

Nayman leaned back in his chair, not believing he had to listen to this. Bobby made an elaborate show of examining his fingernails. Sad to say, when it came to gender issues, Bernie Nayman and Bobby Victory were dinosaurs. Jerry continued, however, undeterred.

"When I was supposed to pick up the bag for you guys last week at the site, Sam, she told me she needed the car for something. And I don't have to tell you, things got a bit heated between us, and she hid them."

"She hid them," Nayman repeated, stoically.

"Yeah. The keys. So, I couldn't get there in time, and the whole thing got messed up, that's what happened."

Nayman studied Jerry like he was looking at an insect. "Jerry, you're a fucking moron," he said. He turned from Jerry to Ted, who lowered his eyes, not wanting to get involved. Nayman shook his head slowly, like he was trying to clear his mind of some oppressive thought. At last, almost reluctantly, he turned back to Jerry.

"Here are your options," he said, in a new, reasonable tone. He raised one finger pedantically. "Number one: I roll you up to the neck in a carpet, stuff you in the back of a sedan and light you on fire with gasoline. You with me?"

Jerry nodded.

"Choice one, all right?" Nayman repeated. He held up a second finger. "Number two. You like sex and travel? You like having sex? You like to travel?"

Jerry nodded. It was hard to deny that so far choice two was sounding like a definite improvement over choice one.

"You get your ass on a flight to Mexico," Nayman went on. "All the ten-dollar hookers you can shake your stick at. You pick up a pistol that belongs to Margolese. So—what's it gonna be?"

Jerry glanced at the passport in his hand. "I was under the impression, you know, with Mr. Margolese getting out and all, that the last job was my last . . ."

"You fucked up that job," Nayman told him.

"You fucked up that job, Jerry," Bobby Victory parroted.

"*This* will be your last job," Nayman said.

"Yeah, but a trip right now. Things are, y'see, difficult," Jerry complained.

Nayman sighed and shook his head. "He called and *asked* for you. Do you want me to call him back in the cell block and let him know you can't go? Because I'll call. I'd love to."

Jerry began to stammer. "No, it's just—"

"You have an arrangement," Nayman interrupted, reminding Jerry of his obligations.

"An *arrangement*, Jerry," threw in Bobby Victory.

"I understand but—"

"Should I call him right now?" Nayman suggested. He smiled coldly when Jerry did not answer. "You're going on a fucking trip, Jerry. The town's called San Miguel. You look for a kid in a hotel, the El Alamo."

Jerry sighed, thinking of what Sam was going to say about this. To put it bluntly, Sam was going to be furious.

"This is a simple fucking task!" Nayman interrupted, throwing a pad and a pen at Jerry, narrowly missing his chest. "Write it down! Roll up your sleeves, for Christ's sake! Get involved!"

Reluctantly, Jerry reached for the pad and pen on the floor. Unfortunately, Ted was reaching at the same time and they banged heads. Bernie Nayman rolled his eyes at this comedy, disgusted.

"The kid's name is Beck," he said slowly, like he was speaking to an idiot.

Jerry dutifully wrote the name on the pad: B-E-C-K. "He's got this particular gun and he's waiting on you," Nayman continued. "When you find him, you bring him and the gun back stateside, to me. You got it?"

"Last chance, Jerry. I'm telling you, the *last*. Even he's getting tired of your shit—he told me so."

"I'll take care of it, Bernie," Jerry managed.

Nayman reached into a drawer and slapped a plane ticket down on his desk.

"*Vaya con dios*, motherfucker," he said. "You're in coach. And, Ted . . . stick around."

It was plain that the meeting was over.

Three

Two hours later, Jerry Welbach stood on the sidewalk outside his apartment complex watching a suitcase—*his* suitcase—sail down from a second-story balcony to the ground. He had to dodge his falling wardrobe to avoid being hit.

"What are you doing?" he shouted upward.

Samantha leaned over the balcony railing and glared down at him. Jerry's face softened slightly: she was beautiful when she was angry, glowing with heat and passion. But she looked like she meant business.

"You said it was your last job, Jerry!"

"Sam, what do you want me to do? Tell him sorry, I can't facilitate that request at this time because the old lady wants me to quit?"

"Something exactly like that," she agreed.

"I'm not in insurance," he explained. But unfortunately, she knew that already; Jerry knew that already; Jerry's profession was the major part of the problem between them. A sneaker flew out the window and Jerry scampered out onto the street to collect it.

"You get on that plane, Jerry, you'll never see me again. Never, ever, never. We talked about this and I told you, I want us to go to Las Vegas. For *me*—but, oh, yeah, that's a laugh, isn't it? As if you'd ever think about anyone besides yourself!"

"You're overreacting," he suggested, trying to calm things down.

"Don't you do that! *Don't* diminish my needs."

"I have to go down there. These things take time, honey."

"I, I, I," she taunted. "I'd like to hear what the group would say about *that*, Jerry."

"How can you use that against me? We're not even married yet, but I go, don't I? The whole group thinks we're married—they gave us the potato slicer, which I graciously accepted, for our anniversary, right? I go along."

"That's it: you go along!" she shouted. "You don't want to get married to me and this is the way you're dealing with it. Back to your same old selfish, self-serving, vile, disgusting self!"

This was getting to be embarrassing.

"Excuse me," he said, "but you're missing the grand design here. If I don't go do this, I'm dead. And it's kinda hard to continue a relationship if I'm stuffed with straw and formaldehyde. If anyone is being selfish . . ."

"Now you blame-shift?" she asked.

This was starting to get to him, it truly was. "Would you gimme a break with the analyzing group terminology?" he shouted.

"You blame-shift! You're a shifter, Jerry, and I'm calling a time-out."

Time-out was the magic phrase with the group they were attending, and they both stopped screaming immediately. Jerry walked around in little circles on the sidewalk, trying to think his way clear. He wanted to be fair. Sam had been pushing to move to Las Vegas for several years now, to get a job in a casino where she believed she could have a fascinating, fulfilling career and also makes lots of money. Jerry had been putting her off, insisting that he already made okay money in Los Angeles, so why should they move? She countered that this was not the point; *she* had a right to a life as well. So somehow it had become a *his* thing and a *her* thing, growing more emotionally charged than merely the choice between staying in L.A. or moving to Nevada. A few weeks ago he had finally agreed to the move. In fact, he had promised. But now this new thing with Nayman had come up and Jerry was in a real bind, like he couldn't win for losing.

"I want you to acknowledge that my needs mean nothing to you," Sam continued, more calmly. "And that you're a selfish prick and a liar."

He sighed and tried to reason with her. "Okay, I'll acknowledge that I promised I'd go to Las Vegas with you. But now we're slightly delayed. If you wanna construe my wanting to stay alive as being selfish, fine. But I have every intention of going with you. In fact, your needs are very important to me."

She stared at him and Jerry sensed maybe he was making a little progress.

"Come on, honey," he pleaded. "Lookit my stuff here all over the street."

She shook her head, an almost resigned look on her face. "I'm going, with or without you, Jerry."

"Come on!"

"What's it gonna be?" she insisted. "And I swear to God, I'm serious this time."

Jerry didn't know what to do. He stood there helplessly. Finally, he shrugged his shoulders.

"Bastard!" she said scornfully.

"Bastard? Who was that calling me baby, calling me sweetheart, just last night? Don't you remember?"

"Jerry," she said, "the only thing I'm interested in calling you is a cab."

And then his wallet came flying down from the balcony. It hit Jerry on the forehead with a loud smack.

Four

The plane ticket Bernie Nayman had given him left
LAX at 2:47 that afternoon, so there wasn't time for
regrets. Jerry got with the program and joined the
excruciatingly plodding world of jet travel: a cab to
the airport, checking in, waiting in line, more waiting
at the departure gate. The boredom was soothing to
a guy who had just lost his girlfriend. All in all, he
was glad to be in motion, however slowly, between
one place and another, flying through the big dreamy
nowhere of clouds and empty space.

The flight to Toluca, the closest airport to San Miguel, took two and a half hours. The plane was
crowded with people, about three-quarters gringo
and one-quarter Mexican families and business-
people going home. The gringos tended to be young
and revved up, dressed in surfer shorts and party

clothes. Gringos go to Mexico to party, bust loose, and take part in things that they aren't allowed to do back home.

The plane came down with a chirp upon the tarmac, and here he was: Mexico. The atmosphere changed immediately, walking out of the plane into blinding sunlight, down metal steps that had been wheeled against the side of the jet, like you saw in old movies. The airport buildings were hardly more than a few low shacks, the desert and the mountains in the distance. The heat from the sun made Jerry feel like having a siesta, getting laid, and drinking a whole lot more *cerveza*, all at once.

Jerry went through customs, retrieved his bag, and wandered into the terminal. Since he had to make a call, he headed past two serious-looking officials and toward a phone bank. Jerry picked up the receiver, completely baffled as to how to make a call. Scanning the instruction sheet proved useless: it was entirely in Spanish, a language that Jerry had never had the time or inclination to pick up.

An automated operator on the line chimed in, telling Jerry in Spanish to enter his pin number. Totally lost, Jerry began punching a few numbers. Inevitably, the operator's voice began to instruct him to review the following menu choices and to select the appropriate number to continue with his card. Hopelessly confused, Jerry scanned the terminal for someone—anyone—who could perhaps help a stranger in a strange land make a simple call. But everyone in the terminal was rushing off, eager to get out of the airport. They didn't notice the poor gringo with the phone to his ear and a dazed expression on his face.

Knowing it was hopeless, Jerry hung up the phone, then spotted the car-rental desks at the other end of the terminal. Jerry made his way to the counter, where a friendly car-rental rep—who thankfully spoke perfect English—helped set him up with a car.

"All set, Mr. Welbach," the rental rep said with a smile. He was a good-looking young guy with a mustache and a bright shirt. "If you go to the front there, a shuttle will pick you up and take you to you car."

"What kind of car is it exactly?"

"It's a Chrysler. New, sir." Jerry wasn't enthused. "Is there a problem, Mr. Welbach?"

"Look, it's my first time to Mexico," Jerry confided to the rep. "And well, a Chrysler? I drive a Chrysler in America."

The car rep nodded understandingly. He had met gringos like this before, by the planeload.

"I just thought . . . I don't know . . . Would you happen to have anything a little more *authentic*, a little more, uh . . ."

"Mexican?" finished the rep.

"Exactly, yeah. Get into the spirit," Jerry agreed.

"Let's see what we can do for you. Your first time—wow, exciting. *Habla español, Señor Welbach?"*

Jerry grinned back, not knowing what the fuck the guy said, but liking the sound of it.

"I didn't think so. Just what you learned on Speedy Gonzales, eh?" the rep said in Spanish, amused. Switching back to English, he said, "I think I have exactly what you want. An El Camino," he told Jerry, laying on an extra thick accent.

"Yeah, that's good. Excellent."

The rep gave Jerry his paperwork and pointed him toward a golf cart shuttle.

"I get the feeling you're going to get into a lot of trouble here, sir," the rep said in Spanish with a sigh as soon as Jerry was out of earshot.

"Raoul!" he called out, summoning a mechanic to take Jerry to his new car. Raoul, a young man in his twenties wearing oil-stained coveralls and standing in the car-rental lot just outside the rental desk, looked at the side door, where Jerry was standing.

Raoul turned to the group of other mechanics who were sitting on garbage bins, taking a smoke break in the hot sun. Raoul motioned to Jerry and said in Spanish to his compadres, "Who wants him? A two-dayer. He looks like a lead foot and a brake-rider."

The other mechanics suddenly leapt to their feet, fishing around in their pockets for their keys, eagerly handing them to Raoul. Raoul knew there was only one way to settle this.

"No, no, come on. Count of three." The three mechanics held out their fists, bobbing them up and down to the count of three. On three, they shot fingers out. "Okay, Mañuel," Raoul said, declaring the winner of the hand game. Mañuel tossed his keys to Raoul and went back to polishing a distributor cap as Raoul walked toward Jerry with a smile on his face.

Jerry roared out of the rental lot in a midnight-blue El Camino with a personalized license plate that said, "Mañuel." It was very authentic, a machine that rumbled with a deep bass growl as it ate up the road. He liked it that he wouldn't be a conspicuous *norte Americano*. With wheels like this, he knew he'd fit right in.

The highway opened up in a vast nothingness of

desert and mountains. Jerry turned on the radio and was feeling pretty damn good. He only wished Sam could see him being such a free spirit in a foreign land. He passed fields and farms as the rumbling engine propelled the El Camino down the road. There were burros and peasant farmers in baggy clothes and little children that he waved to. As the afternoon progressed, the mountains grew steadily closer. After a while, he started singing along to the radio, making up his own words instead of Spanish or just singing out "El Camino." It was very liberating to sing at the top of his lungs with the windows open and the warm Mexican air caressing his skin. It made him feel like a new person.

Jerry eventually pulled up to a crossroads in the middle of the stark landscape. The midst of the desert seemed an awkward place for a stoplight, but nonetheless, Jerry waited patiently for the light to turn green. It was taking an inordinately long time to change. Looking both ways, he could see no cars along the stretch of asphalt in either direction.

Growing impatient, Jerry eased the El Camino out a little into the intersection so he could see more clearly over a slight rise in the highway to his left. But an old trailer billboard obstructed the view even more from his new vantage point. As Jerry eased the car out a little farther, he could finally see that the way was clear, and he stepped on the gas.

Suddenly, a truck's horn blasted as it swerved around Jerry, having sped up through the intersection to Jerry's right. Caught completely off guard, Jerry slammed on the brakes as the tuck swept by, barely missing the front end of the El Camino.

Swallowing hard, Jerry fought to control his heart, which was now hammering in his throat. That was too close. Finally, the light turned green, and Jerry carefully guided the car across the intersection.

Many more miles down the road, Jerry stopped to ask directions from an old woman who was standing with a herd of goats by the side of the road. She didn't have many teeth in her mouth, and she didn't speak a word of English. But somehow Jerry managed to communicate with her, using gestures and mime. She was very friendly and warm. Sam would have liked her, he thought absently.

He drove on and soon he was in the foothills of the mountains. He went through a long tunnel, and by the time he got out the other side it was night. A darker, more velvety kind of night than you got in L.A. *Real* night, it seemed to Jerry. Half an hour later he was pulling into the outskirts of San Miguel, a village of low buildings and narrow cobblestone streets. The houses were very poor, half falling down and faded, and yet Jerry found the village picturesque, like a faded postcard. There were banners and hanging decorations, candles flickering in the windows of darkened houses. But he didn't see any people. It was almost eerie.

He kept driving. He was wondering where all the people were when he turned a corner and saw three small children run across the road with sparklers. They were laughing and singing and Jerry was starting to get the idea that there was some kind celebration going on. A fiesta. Soon he came to the main square, the plaza, and suddenly there was a whole crowd running with sparklers, screaming and calling out. One of the men was dressed in a bull's head with hundreds of firecrackers fixed to his costume. He startled Jerry by running right in front of the car, practically bouncing off of the hood before tearing off after the revelers. Jerry continued driving slowly through the crowd. There were people everywhere now, music in the streets. Some of the men were shooting pistols into the air. Maybe it was a national holiday, like the 4th of July. People seemed to know how to have fun in Mexico, which was okay with Jerry.

Just when he thought he was lost, Jerry saw a two-story building up ahead that appeared to be a small hotel and bar. "EL AL MO" was painted on one side of the building, faded with time, missing a letter. Jerry pulled into a dirt parking lot, alongside some very old cars and trucks, as well as several mules and horses that were tied to posts. Near the entrance to the bar, several drunk men were shouting and shooting pistols into the sky.

Jerry had arrived. Now he only had to meet the kid named Beck, and get the old gun that Margolese wanted. It seemed pretty simple, but in the last five years, Jerry had learned not to take any chances. He opened his bag next to him on the passenger seat of the El Camino and searched through his spare underwear, socks, and shirts. He found what he was after, pulling out what looked like a sandwich wrapped in tinfoil. But it was no sandwich. He unwrapped a black, paint-chipped snub-nose .38 with the bullets out, loose. He loaded six bullets into the chamber. Spinning the cylinder, he fumbled around with the bullets, finally managing to stuff the gun into his waistband. As he confidently strode toward the bar, the gun fell out and clattered to the street. His cheeks reddening, Jerry scooped up the gun and secured it again, making sure it wouldn't slip.

At last, ready for anything, though more than a little apprehensive, he walked into the bar.

Five

It wasn't like any bar Jerry had ever entered in Los Angeles. It looked like anything could happen here. Anything at all. The place was dark and filled almost entirely with men, most of them extremely drunk. Jerry felt a marked drop in the volume as he walked through the door. A number of bleary, hostile eyes turned his way.

He made his way toward the bar, hoping to avoid a confrontation. The bartender was a florid man in his fifties with a large, drooping mustache. He stared at Jerry warily as he approached, like he was saying, "You are in the wrong place, America." Jerry got the message, loud and clear; in fact, he would have been glad to turn around and leave, if that were possible. A few people brushed against him hard, dangerously. Jerry ignored them, squeezing into a spot at the bar.

"This is the El Alamo?" he asked the bartender.

"Yeah, it is," the bartender told him, not even making an effort to be friendly. "What do you want here?"

"A drink. Tequila."

The florid man reached very slowly for the bottle, never taking his eyes off Jerry. Jerry sensed he had a problem here.

"The reason I ask is, no one like you ever comes to this town," the bartender confided. "It's death, this town. Nothing here but farmers and *banditos*, and I don't see a hoe. You a *bandito*, America?"

Jerry smiled vaguely, leaving the question hanging in the air. He glanced around the room while the bartender poured a huge shot of tequila for the gringo.

"No, huh? Okay, maybe you came for the sunshine?" the bartender asked, not able to restrain his curiosity. "There is plenty of that. Too much of it, if you—"

"I'm looking for Señor Beck," Jerry interrupted him, clumsily pulling out a fifty dollar bill and letting it sit on the bar. The bartender glanced at the bill, then looked up to give Jerry a blank stare.

The bartender reached for the fifty dollar bill and nodded toward a crowded table in the back of the room.

There were several men and women seated at the back table in a haze of cigarette smoke, with a nearly empty bottle of tequila and shotglasses scattered around. All of them were as drunk as everybody else in the bar. Jerry had no trouble picking out Beck, the lone gringo, who was the most inebriated of the lot. He was in his early twenties, just a kid really. Probably he had been nice looking once, before he had turned partying south of the border into a major pursuit.

"Hi," Jerry said, walking over.

All conversation immediately stopped as everyone at the table stared at him with surprised, wobbly eyes, like he was a visitor from outer space. The man closest to Beck staggered to his feet and gave Jerry a look of murderous intent. Maybe he was Beck's bodyguard, or just a violent friend.

Jerry blanched, not knowing what to do. So he grabbed a nearby chair and took a seat, saying in what he hoped was a nonchalant tone, "Is this seat taken?" No one responded. Jerry gulped.

"I know who you are," Beck said at last, slurring his words.

"That'll make things a little easier," Jerry agreed.

All of the men at the table glared at Jerry. They looked as if they were ready to pounce. Sweating,

Jerry motioned to the .38 tucked in his waistband, hoping that he was coming off as confidently as Steve McQueen. Beck turned to the men and spoke to them in Spanish, saying, "It's okay. I know what this man wants. He has the right to be here." Everybody at the table visibly relaxed. Beck motioned for Jerry pull his chair closer.

"Want a drink?" he asked.

"All right."

Beck poured himself and Jerry a shot of tequila from the nearly empty bottle on the table. He grinned at Jerry sloppily and downed his glass in a single swallow. Jerry drank more slowly, sensing it was a good idea to keep his wits about him.

"So I guess you wanna see it?"

"I'm gonna have to," Jerry told him.

Beck spoke to one of the men, who handed him a dirty knapsack. He pulled out an old oilcloth with something the size of a banana wrapped in it. He was about to open the oilcloth, but he looked around the rowdy bar and apparently thought better of it.

"Come with me," he said, standing up uncertainly from the table and leading the way into the men's room in back. Beck locked the door behind them as best as he could and leaned against a sink that looked as if it was occasionally used as a urinal. As rest rooms went, this one did not meet strict *Good Housekeeping* sanitary standards. But Beck didn't seem to notice. Slowly, he unraveled the oilcloth to reveal the antique gun inside.

"This is what they call the Mexican," Beck said, smiling crazily.

Jerry stared at the gun in fascination. It was very old and beautiful, a flintlock pistol made from silver and gold and polished wood. Beck handed the gun to Jerry, who took it carefully. It was heavier than it looked.

"Sure is pretty," Jerry said.

"You shitting me? Yeah, it's pretty!" Beck laughed. "It was made for a wealthy landowner, a nobleman, by a poor Mexican gunsmith. He fashioned this gun as a gift to go along with the hopes that the nobleman's son would take his only daughter's hand in marriage."

Jerry nodded, checking out the beautifully crafted pistol, losing himself in the tale Beck began to relate.

San Miguel's dusty streets stood quiet in anticipation. Not a bird chirped, and the wind even ceased stirring the chaparral by the side of the rough road that led into town. Everyone was waiting for the gunsmith.

The gunsmith was almost ready. The townspeople had

waited three months to catch their first glimpse of the pistol he was currently working on. Finally, the day had come. All the people in the village gathered in the choked square and waited in anticipation, standing beneath the burning sun, talking excitedly among themselves.

At last, a hush fell upon the crowd as the gunsmith walked out of his shop into the square with the pistol in his hand. He raised the gun high for everybody to see. No one had ever laid eyes on a more beautiful gun. The people went wild. They sighed at its beauty. It was everything they thought it would be. Some even thought it was too beautiful to look at, its burnished surface glinting in the harsh sunlight. After the initial excitement died down just a little, the gunsmith motioned to a young man in the crowd to come and be the first to shoot this wonderful weapon. The young man couldn't believe his good fortune to be picked out for such a honor. His mother and grandmother were standing next to him, very proud their boy was selected. They both kissed him and congratulated him.

It was considered a huge honor, and it was also considered very good luck to be the first hand that fired a newly fashioned gun. Especially one as beautiful as this, made for the hand of a nobleman.

The lucky young man who had been chosen held the gun and stared at it for a long while, entranced by its flawless craftsmanship. Finally, the gunsmith had to *nudge him and point to a clay pitcher that had been placed on top of a barrel a short distance away. The young man raised the pistol and aimed. The gun was so beautiful, the gold and silver shimmering, that the people in the crowd hardly dared to breathe. Slowly, the young man pulled the wonderfully polished trigger.*

The gun discharged with a terrific blast. But unfortunately, the pistol backfired, killing the young man instantly. He fell to the ground with a horrible thud. Without expression, the gunsmith walked to the young man's corpse, stepped over it, bent down, and retrieved the pistol.

Scratching his head and looking over the pistol, the vexed gunsmith calmly went back to his shop to begin repairs on the faulty gun, while the young man's mother and grandmother ran screaming over the poor boy's body and the town gathered around the figures grieving in the dust.

"Legend is, it's been cursed ever since. Hasn't harmed me any, though," Beck said. "I love to look at it. The thought that this gun has been around so long freaks me out. I mean, you see these things all the fucking time at museums and shit, but it's not the same as walking around with a piece of history in your pocket. Somebody made this a hundred or so years ago. With his fucking hands, man."

Jerry studied the pistol with new appreciation. It seemed to him that flintlock pistols came from a period a lot longer ago than just a hundred years or so, but he had always been vague when it came to history.

"There's a bullet in there," Beck was telling him. "Hand-fucking-made, see? You don't even want to know what this gun is worth."

"You're probably right," Jerry told him. Which reminded him that he had to get this very valuable gun back to Los Angeles right away.

Six

Jerry and Beck staggered out from the El Alamo.

Jerry was only moderately buzzed, but Beck had a big head start and could barely stay on his feet. Outside, the fiesta was in full swing, raucously loud now, with music and screaming and guns firing off like it was the end of the world. The same crowd of guys were standing in the parking lot unloading their pistols at the moon.

Beck careened toward a wall to take a piss, while Jerry continued to where his El Camino was parked nearby, carrying the antique pistol in the oil rag. He tossed the beautiful gun onto the passenger seat and decided he could probably unburden himself of his more modern weapon as well. He took his .38 from his waistband, leaned inside the door, and hid it beneath the dashboard. Meanwhile, Beck was letting loose a river of tequila and beer against the wall, talking at the same time, which probably was not wise in his condition.

"We could *sell* that gun," Beck said out of nowhere. "It's a great fucking gun, man, and I'm not just talking shit either. You don't have to be . . . aaaaawww fuuuuck! I've been pissing on myself! Fuck! . . . Anyway, the Old Man is nothing to be afraid of. As a matter of fact, I just told him last week to fuck off."

"Yeah, you did," Jerry said, leaning against the fender of the El Camino, waiting for Beck to finish up.

"Yeah, I did! You know what I told him? 'Fuck off, you old prune shitass!' If you—"

Suddenly, Beck collapsed with a thud on the ground by the wall. Jerry supposed it was bound to happen, the way Beck had been gulping down tequila. He laughed tolerantly and walked over to the heap of drunken gunrunner on the ground. He nudged Beck with his foot.

"C'mon, fella. Up and at 'em," Jerry urged. "C'mon, man, you're soaked in fucking urine. You gonna make me carry you?"

But Beck was out cold. *Really* cold. Jerry sighed because this was starting to be a drag. He lifted up the kid and staggered with him over to the El Camino. It was amazing how heavy people were when their lights were out. Jerry was breathing hard by the time he set Beck down on the ground by the car. He got the passenger door open, put the antique gun on top of the dash, and with a lot of huffing and puffing, finally managed to get Beck flopped into the front seat. The kid's head hit the back of the white vinyl upholstery, splattering blood. A good amount of blood.

"Jesus! You whacked your noggin," Jerry cried, looking at his own hands to find they were covered with blood also. "Oh, shit!"

Jerry was suddenly sober, wishing that this wasn't happening. He forced himself to check Beck's body in order to figure out where the hell the blood was coming from. He found the source quickly enough. Blood was oozing from a small, neat hole at the very top of Beck's head. Which was *very* odd, when you thought about it. And more odd still: *Beck was fucking dead!* Out of nowhere. One second he was peeing against the wall, talking unwisely about double-crossing Big Boss Margolese. Then the next second, a bullet in the top of his head and he's dead forever.

Jerry stood up completely freaked. A loud volley of gunfire blasted from the plaza. Jerry skittishly hopped around, desperately trying to avoid another phantom bullet, his hands covering his head. A second later, a bullet rained down on the hood of the El Camino. A moment after that, another few bullets landed on the ground nearby, causing small dust clouds in the dirt.

Jerry was starting to get the picture. He scurried around to the driver's door and got himself inside the safety of the car. It was crazy, but Beck had been killed by a bullet from the sky, fired by all these fucking assholes shooting at the moon. What goes up must come down, after all.

Jerry had no idea what the hell he was going to do now that he had a dead guy in the passenger seat and a priceless antique pistol on the dashboard. He shoved the old pistol into the glove compartment and started up the El Camino. There was nothing like death raining down from the sky to get a person out of the fiesta spirit.

Seven

As it happened, this was the *good* part of Jerry Welbach's night in the town of San Miguel. The bad part was still to come.

Jerry left the El Alamo parking lot and drove to the first pay phone he saw—outside a gas station. The attendant was a middle-aged man with sad eyes, seated on a rickety wood chair near his single pump. He watched as Jerry picked up the pay phone, and began to frantically dial a number he knew by heart, gambling that he had put enough change into the phone slot. Miraculously, he had.

Ted answered on the second ring, but the connection was terrible. Jerry covered his ear in order to hear better, but it was like trying to talk to Antarctica in the middle of a blizzard.

"Ted, wait a minute. Stop talking for a second. You

keep cutting in," Jerry told him. "Yes, I found the gun. I found it."

"It's in your possession?"

"As we speak. But, like I told you, there's a little problem."

"The kid gave you the slip?" Ted was noisily eating something, a midnight snack, which didn't help matters, communication-wise. "He's a souse, that kid. Go to another bar and you'll find him," Ted advised.

Jerry only wished it was that easy. "The kid's dead. . . . Teddy, did you hear me?"

Ted had stopped eating. There was a significant pause from the Los Angeles end. "Yeah, I heard you," he said finally. "How?"

"Bad luck. There's all kinds of people shooting goddamn guns off, up into the sky and all around the fucking place. It's Independence Day here. National holiday or something. He got tagged in the head from one those bullets on its way down. He's dead. The little fucker is in my car, right now, *dead*!"

"Jeez, Jerry, that's not a little problem—that's a *big* problem. That little fucker is Margolese's grandson."

"What? *What*? You're kidding me!"

"No, I am not kidding you," Ted assured.

Jerry clutched the phone, cursing his usual shitty luck. Either way, he was royally fucked. *A bullet from the sky, for chrissake!*

"Aw you really fucked it this time," Ted told him sadly.

"How did *I* have anything to do with it? One minute the kid's pissing on himself; the next minute he's got a mouthful of concrete!"

"Don't even move," Ted told him. "I'm calling in right now. We'll get me on a plane and help you straighten this shit out."

"Jesus, Ted. What should I do? Maybe I should call Nayman?"

"Yes . . . no. Jeez, no. I guess I should get down there myself and explain it to Nayman, Jerry. I'll get dressed and go down there. Just sit tight."

"Ted, you get word to the Old Man, okay? Tell him I didn't even know who the kid was, all right? . . . Ted? . . . Ted! . . . Hello!"

But the line to the City of the Angels had gone dead. Jerry took a deep breath, trying to be philosophical and think through this rationally. Then he smashed the receiver against the phone.

As he did, something outside the phone booth caught Jerry's eye. As he turned to look in that direction, his eyes widened in horror: a very spiffy fire engine–red S.S. Nova hot rod was idling beside the El Camino, and a young Mexican in his early twenties was hanging out the passenger window of the Nova, watching his friend hot-wiring Jerry's car.

The El Camino's engine suddenly roared to life.

"Oh, no," Jerry breathed. He scrambled to open the phone booth door, fumbling with the latch while both cars peeled out and accelerated off into the night. Jerry swore as he watched Beck's body, his gun, his wallet with all the cash he had in the world, and most important, the antique pistol, race out of sight.

Jerry's knees were weak. He sat down on the curb, miserable, wondering what he was going to do now. *Maybe* Old Man Margolese might have forgiven the death of his grandson if Jerry had been able to produce the priceless pistol he had been sent to Mexico to fetch. Without the pistol, he was totally fucked. Jerry felt like crying—he truly did—because this was the end of the road, failure with a capital F.

He sat there for a long time, feeling like the most unhappy person on earth. Then he heard a sad sound: *heeee-haaawwww.* It was a donkey braying, staring at him, attached to a small cart about twenty feet down the road. Burro, he supposed, was the

Spanish word. The burro brayed again: *heeeee-haaawwww*. It was the most pathetic, desolate sound he had ever heard.

But it gave Jerry an idea.

Eight

Samantha Barzel was cruising in her green VW Beetle on the wide open freeway to Las Vegas, riding to a new life.

She was still in California, but it was not part of any California she knew. The freeway was straight and monotonous, cutting like a knife through a desert that was brown and barren and empty as death. Sam had the radio blaring to keep her awake, with Nancy Sinatra singing "These Boots Were Made for Walking"—quite apt, when Sam thought about it. This was a *journey*, she told herself, more than a mere trip. Every now and then she caught sight of her own reflection in her rearview mirror. Men used to tell her that she was beautiful, before she got hooked up with that selfish shithead Jerry, wasting herself. She still looked pretty good, she thought.

A sign on the side of the road gave her a mileage update: LAS VEGAS 198. Just the thought of so many miles was starting to make her drowsy. When she couldn't drive anymore, she pulled off on a freeway exit, toward a shopping mall on the side of the road. Sam liked shopping malls, all the hustle and bustle, the concourse of human interchange. She parked in the vast lot and made her way through the vaulted exterior until she found the food court. She bought a Tab from one of the fast-food counters and sat on a plastic bucket seat at a brightly colored plastic table, leafing through a hardcover book she had brought along for inspiration: *Selfish Men and the Women Who Love Them*. This book had become her Bible the last few months, and was very revealing about a whole lot of issues.

Engrossed as she was in personal revelations, Sam did not notice the well-dressed black man, ultrahip with designer glasses, who was standing at the lip of the food court watching her intently. Nor did she see the white man sitting at a competing establishment at the opposite side of the food court, who was keeping an eye on both the black man *and* Sam. The white man in his mid-thirties, not dressed so well, or so hip. His clothes looked as though they had been bought off the rack at Kmart. His head was nearly bald except for some tufts at the side; he had a well-sculptured goatee and looked a little nebbishy.

Sam drank her soft drink and read, not aware that she had acquired a retinue. Her entire concentration was focused on her book, and the many truths that were written therein about women who allowed themselves to become victims of men, loving too much. She kept nodding because it was as if the author had been peeping in on her and Jerry, and taking notes. The book was that right on.

Sam finished a chapter and closed the book, freshly inspired. She was ready for Las Vegas now. Ready for anything. But first she needed to pee. She stood from the orange plastic table, disposed of her empty cup in the provided receptacle, and made her way across the food court, past Sears and Radio Shack, until she came to a long corridor between Foot Locker and Barnes and Noble, where there was a sign pointing to the men's and ladies' rest rooms. The well-dressed black man followed her, trailing about twenty feet back. And behind him stalked the white man, farther back still.

The ladies' room was empty when Sam walked inside. She passed the two sinks and made her way into one of the metal cubicles, closing and locking the door behind her. As she peed, Sam heard the main rest room door open and someone walk to the sink. The black man had grabbed a CLOSED FOR CLEANING sign from a nearby cleaning cart and hung it on the restroom doorhandle, before quietly slipping inside. She flushed the toilet, opened the cubicle door, and nearly had a heart attack. The well-dressed black man with expensive glasses was giving her a hard look, his gun drawn.

Before she could react, he covered Sam's mouth with his hand and pushed her back into the stall. Sam was terrified now, whimpering. He locked the door behind him, motioning her to be quiet.

"You need to know that I don't stand for any shit," he said. "You're gonna stop crying, lady, and you're gonna walk out of here with me. You got that?"

Sam nodded, her eyes wide.

"I knew you would behave yourself." The black man seemed very sure of himself. But just as they were about to leave the stall, they heard the main door to the rest room open. There was a surge of sound, as the open door let in the canned music and the cacophony of voices of the people milling about the mall. Sam expected the door to close and the outside sounds to become muted once again, but the door did not close. This seemed a little strange.

The man put his finger to his mouth, hushing Sam. They both waited in silence, listening very carefully. But there was nothing to hear. No sink running, no toilet flushing, no footsteps. Nothing. The black man frowned with concern. He gestured for her to sit on the toilet seat, and she obeyed him instantly. He unlocked the stall door and opened it very slowly, inch by inch until he could see out into the rest room. But the rest room was empty. There was nobody. He saw that the main door had been propped open with a wedge and the CLOSED FOR CLEANING sign had been turned around to let people know the facilities, in fact, were open.

The black man relaxed visibly, understanding the situation. He motioned Sam out of the stall, walked to the door, turned the sign back around so that people would think the rest room was closed, then kicked out the doorstop. He was facing Sam at the sink as the heavy door hissed slowly shut behind him.

Sam gulped and couldn't believed her eyes. As the door shut, she saw that there was a white man standing behind it. The white man had a gun in his hand, with a long silencer attached to the barrel. She had never seen so many guys with guns in a ladies' room—or anywhere, for that matter—before.

Meanwhile, the black man was trying to quiet her down, his back to the white man, unaware that they weren't alone. Sam was feeling very, very nervous, just trying to breathe, staring over the black man's shoulder at the white man with the gun.

The black man's expression changed. He seemed to read his own peril in Sam's frightened eyes.

"As I was saying . . ." he began. Midsentence, he spun around with lighting speed, raising his gun. But the black man didn't have a chance. All he could do was hold up his hand, as though this would stop anything. The man in the white shirt began firing, his silenced gun making little hollow plipping sounds. A bullet ripped through the black man's hand. Sam screamed at the top of her lungs.

For Sam, everything that ensued happened in an incoherent confusion of events. The black man fell on her, pushing her back into the stall, blood flowing from his wound. He was still alive. He tried to raise his gun, helplessly, but it was no use. The white man just kept firing and firing, unloading his clip. Sam could feel the black man's body jerk as each shot hit. She closed her eyes and screamed in terror. Then the white man was grabbing her, yanking her hard, pulling her out from underneath the black man, who was clearly dead. She tried to fight the killer off, but he was too strong for her. He dragged her halfway across the bathroom and gave her a hard shake, doing his best to calm her.

"You're going to live, maybe, if you do *exactly* like I say. You understand what I'm saying?"

Sam nodded. All she really heard was, "You're going to live." *Maybe.*

The burro clipped-clopped along the dark country highway, not a speedy mode of transportation by any means. Jerry's kidneys were jounced with every step, and after a few hours, his knees felt permanently bowed. Without question, donkey travel was a pain in the ass.

Heee-haaaw!

Every twenty minutes or so, the fucking burro felt some weird compulsion to bray. Jerry was not amused. He came down slowly out of the foothills. Dawn was just breaking when he entered the long tunnel that he had whizzed through last night so quickly in his rental car, coming the other way. By the time he emerged from the far end of the tunnel into the desert, the morning was full-fledged. Jerry was exhausted, dirty, hot, and hungry. He would have exchanged the burro for a burrito in an instant. For the last hour, it seemed to him that the animal had been going slower and slower. Finally, about a hundred yards outside the exit of the tunnel, the burro simply stopped and no amount of kicking or urging would make it move again.

Jerry climbed off of the burro and sighed at the folly of life. The burro blinked at him sleepily. Jerry patted the poor thing good-bye and took off walking down the road. At least there should be traffic now, with the brightening day, and he thought he might be able to hitchhike. He had only walked a dozen feet when he heard a sound behind him, a sputtering engine coming out of the tunnel. He turned to see an ancient chicken truck careening his way, with three peasant farmers in the cab. Jerry put out his thumb and the truck chugged over and stopped.

"Buenos noches," he said. "My car was stolen. Can you give me a lift to the next town?"

The farmers shook their heads at him and laughed. They didn't understand a word of what he was saying, but they seemed to enjoy the spectacle of a woebegone gringo in distress.

Jerry tried again, speaking very slowly. "I need a lift in your truck-o to the next village-o. *Pueblo!* No money . . . no car . . . no *dinero.*"

"Robert DeNiro?" the farmer closest to the window said with a huge grin.

Jerry tied pantomime. He pulled out his pants pockets revealing nothing but some coins. He held an imaginary steering wheel and made little putt-putt sounds. The farmers in the cab of the truck were starting to become concerned. They talked over the situation in low voices among themselves.

"Can you take me to the next town?" Jerry asked again. "Car. Automobila. Pueblo."

"*Sí! Sí!*" said the farmer closest to him, motioning to the back of the truck. "*Vamanos, Señor DeNiro!*"

Nine

By midmorning, the sun blazed down, the air thick with blinding heat and dust. Jerry rode in the back of the pickup surrounded by crates of chickens, dozing when the road wasn't too rough. The peasant farmers in the cab gave him a jug of water and some tortillas to eat.

The truck didn't move very much faster than the burro had. They clunked along at a stately speed that did not upset the chickens. Late in the morning, the farmers left him off at the next village, which wasn't much of anything—only a few buildings that looked like they were falling apart in slow motion in the sun. Jerry was standing in the town plaza, wondering what to do next, when he noticed an automobile junkyard just a little ways down the dusty road. He walked toward it sluggishly. He had been in Mexico less than twenty-four hours, but he was learning that things did not move quickly here, particularly one's own feet.

The junkyard was a walled enclosure full of rusted engine parts and disembodied fenders and doors. Jerry was about to give up his idea when he noticed an old Ford pickup that had four tires, two doors, and seemed to possess all the required parts, including an ugly dog that was sitting in the flatbed in back with a deflated football in its teeth, staring at Jerry with curiosity. The truck had once been a cream color with orange trim, but that was a long time ago, way before Jerry was born. Still, there was something about the old pickup that appealed to him. It had a certain retro style, very 1950s.

Jerry turned and found a wizened old man watching him from the shade of a tin shed. He seemed to be the proprietor of this automobile graveyard.

It wasn't much like buying a car in Los Angeles, but Jerry needed wheels. Now came the tricky part: money. Unfortunately, Jerry didn't have any, except a few stray coins in his pocket. He took off his wristwatch, handed it to the old man, and pointed once again at the truck. The old man frowned, obviously hoping for cash. Nevertheless, he examined the watch closely, and held it up to his ear in order to listen to it tick.

In this manner, they soon had a deal. At last the old man put the watch on his own scrawny wrist and rose from his spot in the shade to accompany Jerry to his new vehicle. The brown junkyard dog was still in the back of the truck, slathering over the football in his mouth. Which presented a slight problem. The dog only glared back at him, refusing to move. It was the scruffiest, meanest-looking brown dog Jerry had ever seen, missing a number of teeth—though the teeth it had left were worrisome.

"You got a rabid dog out here! You gotta do something about this!" Jerry ordered. But the dog didn't move. Jerry reached to touch him, but this proved to be a mistake; the dog snarled and almost bit his hand off. The proprietor laughed and shook his head, no, no, no. Then he walked around to the cab, pulled out a leash, and handed it to Jerry, indicating that the dog went with the truck.

Ten

Sam was in shock. The white man led her out of rest room, staying close. He had put his gun away but his hand was around her arm, gripping hard.

"C'mon, just stay cool, lady," he whispered into her ear. "Easy does it."

They walked down the hallway from the bathroom toward the main concourse of the mall. There was blood on Sam's shirt from the black man who lay leaking on the ladies' room floor. Sam felt unreal, like she was in a dream. People seemed to swell out of her way, some looking at her with concern, but most looking away, not wanting to get involved.

"No, no, help me . . ." Sam pleaded, traumatized, but no one intervened, if they heard her at all.

"You're doing fine, lady, just fine," the man told her encouragingly. They made a sharp left, and before she knew it, they were out the exit and in the parking lot, the sun a white blur of light to her dilated pupils. Sam couldn't get enough oxygen, and she kept gulping air. Years ago, she used to have anxiety attacks just like this. Only then the anxiety was imaginary.

They began walking down an aisle of parked cars. "Fuck it!" he said, stopping short. "Just look at that!"

Sam was beyond comprehension. As far as she could tell, there seemed to be a delivery truck blocking a Lincoln town car. What this meant in the greater scheme of things, she couldn't say.

"Where's your fucking car?" he was asking angrily.

She nodded toward the area where her Beetle was parked and they began walking briskly from the blocked Lincoln toward the H rows. While they were walking, Sam had a cagey idea to pretend not to be able to find her car, which seemed reasonable enough with all these acres of Fords and Toyotas and Volvos and Chevrolets. She wasn't sure what she would gain by this, but any delay seemed an improvement on the basic scenario. Maybe if they walked around long enough, a nice policeman would rescue her. But the man wasn't dumb. He saw the green Beetle right away as they turned the corner of the aisle, and he led her to it. It came as a shock that he knew her vehicle. In fact, he must have been following her all the way from L.A.

"C'mon, the keys," he urged.

Her hand was shaking so badly she couldn't get the keys out of her bag. The man had to do it, taking her purse. He opened the car and shoved her into the passenger seat. He took the wheel, started up the engine, and peeled out of the lot, swerving and nearly missing dozens of cars as he recklessly guided the car back on the freeway ramp toward Las Vegas.

"Are you hurt?" he asked.

Sam was crying again. "No . . . yes. I don't know. . . .*Truck!*" she screamed, pointing at an eighteen wheeler barreling their way. The man swerved to the right and they narrowly missed a collision. Somehow for Sam, this was the last straw. To be kidnapped from a ladies' room, one guy dying on top of her, and now nearly dying herself in a traffic accident—how much more could a person take on any average afternoon?

"Stop! Pull over. I'm gonna be sick!" she told him.

"Hold on to it. Just try'n hold it."

"I can't. It's coming up."

He maneuvered the green Beetle, abruptly changing lanes and heading toward the side of the road, with the horns of other drivers screeching at them. Sam stumbled out of the passenger door and knelt down on the shoulder, grateful for the temporary lack of motion.

"Why? Why don't I listen?" she moaned, not entirely coherent. "She told me: Don't go. I don't like you driving alone on that highway. And I didn't listen. I'll be fine, Ma, it's okay, Ma. But it's not okay, is it? I rolled my eyes—that's what I did. I made a conscious decision not to listen like I always do, and look what happened to me. I'm dead."

"Whoa, whoa, hang on a second here, for fuck's sake. You're not dead. You would've been if I hadn't saved your life," the man told her. "What's the matter with you? Would you rather that it was *you* back there? . . . No, I don't think so."

"Are you gonna kill me?" she asked. Her voice was small and frightened.

He looked at her and sighed. "That all depends on too many variables to answer right now."

More tears were streaming down her face. "Are you gonna rape me?"

"Not likely, no."

"Then, what do you want?"

"I suspect the same thing as that guy back there. The pistol."

Sam looked up at him with stunned eyes, not comprehending.

"The pistol that Jerry's having a hard time coming back from Mexico with all of a sudden," he explained.

"Jerry?"

"I work for Bernie Nayman, who works for Arnold Margolese. Heard of them?"

"Yeah, I heard of them."

"You know, then, that your husband Jerry works for them too, right?"

"No."

"Well, he does."

"No, I know that selfish, no-good, prick liar *works* for them. I meant he's not my husband."

The man in the blue suit stared hard at Sam, down at where she was kneeling on the side of the road. From the expression on his face, he was starting to suspect that this encounter was not going to turn out the way they usually did. It was probably going to get even more complicated.

The man sighed. "Well, whatever he is to you, Jerry is in the shit books," he explained. "It's been known to happen that when people are in shit, they start getting a little skittish about their future, clouds your judgment. There's a lot of people interested in that gun. What we seem to have on our hands here is a 'he who controls the girl controls the pistol' sort of situation."

Sam couldn't believe this was happening.

"I'm a hostage? You just blew that guy to pieces for a fucking *gun*?"

He nodded.

"That's so *Jerry*," she said moodily, looking away. "Look, Jerry and I broke up. If he's doing—I don't know what—it's got nothing to do with me. Okay. Zero."

"You seem like a nice girl," the man said unexpectedly.

"Thank you," she replied with dignity.

"But, it's a fact in life-threatening situations that an individual, no matter what, looks out for number one."

"Life-threatening?"

"I have a gun and you don't know me and I just killed someone else. As a human being you will do or say anything to get out unscathed. That's just how the psyche works."

"So are you gonna kill me?" she asked again.

"If everything turns out fine and Jerry comes through without it all getting funky, I don't think that'll happen, no. If he delivers me the gun, I deliver you to him. So you see, you don't have a single thing to worry about."

Sam shook her head dejectedly. "Great."

"I'm just here to regulate the funkiness."

Eleven

The lonely roadside store was in the middle of nowhere, seemingly in the middle of the harsh Mexican desert, in a small oasis of scruffy trees. Without a map, Jerry wasn't entirely certain where he was. He didn't know how trees could survive in such a land. Personally, he felt wilted. It was midafternoon and he stood at a pay phone in front of the small store, against a sun-baked wall that had painted on it its side CERVEZA FRIA, and below that, in larger letters still: CORONA.

Jerry knew what a Corona was, and he wished he had one. Maybe several.

He held the receiver of the pay phone against his ear, listening to the operator speak to Sam's answering machine.

"I have a collect call for Samantha from Jerry

Welbach?" the operator said. "There's no one there, sir."

"Just give it a second. She's . . . Samsonite, please! Pick up the phone! C'mon, baby, don't do this to me!"

"I'm sorry, sir. Please try again."

"No! Nonononono, *no*! Please, just give it a second. She's—"

Jerry found himself holding a dead telephone, cut off once again. This was getting old, making calls to Sam and never being able to reach her. He slammed the receiver down and was walking back to the Ford pickup when he saw something incredible: a car was barreling down the highway, coming his way. He couldn't believe it. At first it was only a red dot on the horizon, but it gradually grew into a familiar shape; Jerry was almost certain it was the same red Nova that belonged to the two guys who had stolen his car. He rushed to his truck and got behind the wheel. He had left the engine running, but it was a challenge to get into first gear. With a grind of metal, he chugged onto the highway just as the Nova rushed past. It didn't seem possible to chase a souped-up Nova in a beat-up old shitbox truck with a mean junkyard dog riding in the back, but he was determined to try anyway.

The truck farted and popped along at its top speed of forty-five. Despite his determination, Jerry soon saw that it was hopeless. He watched the Nova disappear up ahead on the highway, cursing himself and wondering if his luck would ever change. But then a few minutes later, his luck *did* change. He almost had to pinch himself to make sure he wasn't dreaming. Up ahead on the side of the road, there was a funky little cantina. And in the dirt parking lot outside the cantina, the red Nova was sitting in the sun alongside his stolen El Camino rental.

Jerry grinned. There was nobody else in the parking lot. The thieves were inside the cantina, probably enjoying an ice-cold *cerveza*.

Jerry groped underneath the dashboard, and a big smile lit up his face. His .38 was still there. He tucked the gun into his waistband and walked back to the pickup.

"C'mon, dog," he said, trying to coax the monster hound out from the bed of the truck. But the stubborn dog wouldn't move. Frankly, Jerry was out of patience. He took his gun and pointed it at the dog.

"Out!" he ordered. "Like now, doggie!"

Miraculously, the old brown cur jumped up with his football and left the truck, totally submissive, his tail between his legs. Jerry was starting to enjoy himself. He tucked the gun once more into his waistband and got back into the cab of the Ford. He fastened his seat belt, then accelerated hard, revving the engine. *SMASH!* He drove right into the side of the pristine Nova. It was very satisfying, the sound of tinkling glass and crunching metal. The Nova's horn started blaring like an air-raid siren. Meanwhile, the door of the cantina burst open and the entire clientele of the bar came spilling out into the parking lot to see what was going on. Jerry recognized one of the men, a small, thin guy in his twenties. It was the thief of his El Camino, and the owner of the now-wrecked Nova. His eyes were wide with disbelief at the sight of his demolished car. The thief made his way through the crowd toward Jerry in the truck, seriously pissed off, screaming in Spanish. Jerry slumped over the wheel, pretending to be passed out.

Once the thief was near enough, Jerry whipped out the gun from his waistband and pointed it out the window. The thief stopped with lightning speeding, taken completely by surprise. The crowd ebbed away from Jerry's gun barrel, that swiveled between the thief and the milling onlookers. Jerry stepped out of the pickup and grabbed the thief by his hair, yanking hard.

"*Hola,*" he said. "Where's my stuff? *Pistolero?*"

Jerry demanded. He grabbed his sunglasses off of one of the thief's friends, who was inching away. "Is that my jacket?" Jerry asked another in disbelief. The thief looked at his friend and shrugged. The friend handed Jerry the keys and gave him his jacket too, a little sheepishly.

"Good, where's the gun?" Jerry asked pointedly, cocking back the hammer of his revolver and pressing the barrel against the thief's temple.

"You know what pistol I'm talking about. Now, give!"

The thief began talking in rapid Spanish. Another man came forward from the crowd and reluctantly handed Jerry the antique pistol, still wrapped in its oilcloth.

Jerry nodded, satisfied. Holding on to the thief's hair, he moved them both around toward the El Camino, reached through the window, and put the precious gun into the glove compartment. Once this was taken care of, he aimed his .38 at the Nova and fired, blowing out a tire. He yanked the thief around toward the front of the Nova and shot out the radiator for good measure, setting loose a geyser of hot steam.

Jerry pushed the thief into the front seat of the El Camino. While Jerry made his way around the front of the vehicle to the driver's side, keeping the thief covered with his .38, the old brown dog jumped into the back, refusing to be left behind. Jerry was touched at the devotion.

He fired up the engine and squealed out of the parking lot in a cloud of dust, happier than he had been in a long time.

A hundred miles from Las Vegas, the man in the white shirt drove off the freeway to a gas station, parking by a pay phone at the side of the building.

"What are you doing?" Sam asked.

"We're gonna make a phone call."

"To whom," she said, very primly, feeling fairly uptight.

"Jerry. And we're gonna tell him that Leroy is with you, and for now you're just fine. And then we're gonna hang up."

"*Leroy?*"

"Leroy, that's right."

"That's it?"

"That's enough, believe me. Are you gonna call? Or am I going to have to make you? 'Cuz I will."

"Fine, I'll call. What's the number?"

Leroy stared at her. "*You* have the number."

"I don't! I tell you, I don't know where he is. He's in Mexico. *You* should have the number."

Leroy kept studying her. "You mean to tell me you have no number? A hotel, motel, *nothing*?"

Sam was loosing her patience. "Whatsamatter, don't you listen? We broke up. No longer together. Why would I have a number?"

Leroy appeared uncertain whether to believe her or not. He grabbed her purse and rummaged through it, trying to find an address book, a scrap of paper, something to show she was lying. But there was nothing. Finally, he handed the purse back to her.

"I'm sensing you have trust issues," Sam said sardonically.

Leroy glared at her.

"Satisfied? Can I go to the bathroom now, for chrissake?"

"Okay," he told her. He opened his jacket to show her his gun, a hint to the wise. "Don't talk to nobody, okay?"

Sam walked into the small convenience store, wondering if she could ask the sleepy-looking attendant for help. She didn't think so. Leroy was parked right outside the window, watching her closely. She continued on into the ladies' room and here she found a more promising means of escape: a back window. Sam didn't hesitate. She forced the window open with an angry jerk, climbed up onto the toilet seat, and squeezed herself through. She was lowering herself out the other side onto an oil drum, pleased with herself, when she heard a clicking tongue, mildly disapproving. It was Leroy. He was sitting on another oil drum, watching with a blasé expression on his face.

"This is my profession, you know? I mean, I do this for a living."

She stormed off past him toward the green Beetle, with Leroy on her heels.

"Goody for you," she said.

Twelve

The Nevada desert was even more monotonous than the California desert, just flat, brown, empty land dotted with billboards announcing fabulous jackpots and family fun at the casinos up ahead. Leroy drove at an even 75 mph with Sam in the passenger seat, handcuffed to the door.

"You're wasting your time," she sulked.

"I think I believe you."

She studied him in muted astonishment, trying to figure out this burly man who had killed so easily just a short while ago, and who had kidnapped her. He was a very mild-looking person with his nearly bald head and his real little goatee. Not the way she expected a gangster would look.

He was studying her as well, glancing her way back and forth from the road.

"So what's in Vegas?" he asked.

Sam didn't know why the hell she should tell any of her personal issues to this guy. But it slipped out anyway.

"I'm going to be a waitress. Then I'll make a career as a croupier. They can make a hundred thousand dollars a year. You gotta have the hands, which I do. I got them from my grandmother, Grandma Buck. Which is good too, because my granny Barzel, her hands were like a circus midget's."

He nodded. "Tell me this," he said. "How come you can't live with Jerry?"

"Do you know Jerry?"

Leroy shook his head.

"Jerry has a hard time expressing his feelings," she explained. "He had a real fucked-up childhood. His mother was nuts, y'know, one of those people who thinks the iron's on all the time."

"Don't you love him?"

"That's the problem. I think we love each other too much," she told him. "He's just so *selfish*, y'know. We've been living *his* life forever. He'll tell you another thing altogether, but I give and I give, and he just keeps on taking."

"That's too bad," Leroy told her. He shook his head at the thought of that much altruism.

"Our counselor totally agrees with me, by the way," she continued. "I'm a sensitive, giving person by nature. And he's a hard, cynical taker by nature. That's just a terrible mix, doomed from the outset."

"I don't put stock in those weirdo counselor types," Leroy told her. "All they do is sit around in bare feet and smoke joints."

"Maybe," she agreed, "but that doesn't change the fact that Jerry's a taker and I'm a giver. It's obvious."

"Well, a lot of folks are under the impression that they get to choose who they love," he remarked.

"What are you, taking his side? You *are*! You're a man, and you're taking his side. Of course you are!"

"I'm not taking sides," Leroy objected. "It's bigger than that—you said so yourself. You love him. That's all that matters."

"You really think so?"

"Oh, yeah," he assured her. "Believe me, love is everything."

They drove for the next ten miles without speaking.

"You know, you're a very sensitive person," she said, breaking the silence. "For a cold-blooded killer."

"Thank you, Sam."

Thirteen

Leroy had never met a woman before who had such a miniature bladder. Sam seemed to spend her entire life going from one rest room to another.

So he drove off the freeway yet again, pulling into a gas station/coffee shop/gift store complex that was like a small city of traveling convenience. This time, however, Leroy wasn't letting her out of his sight. He followed her inside the complex, and into the ladies' room itself, locking the door behind them.

Leroy shrugged. "So tell me, what's with this 'we've been living *his* life forever' thing?"

"It's a figure of speech—I didn't mean literally. Jerry's been working for Margolese for five years less a day. Sometimes it just feels lifelong."

"Sounds like jail terms," Leroy told her, studying himself in the bathroom mirror. He could stand losing some weight, particularly in his belly, which was starting to look like he had a bowling ball under his shirt. In his profession, it wasn't so easy to diet, what with the odd hours and the stress.

"It is," Sam was saying from inside her stall. "Arnold Margolese is in jail because Jerry put him there."

"That's how Margolese got sent to jail? What, did he rat him out or something?"

"No, Jerry was coming across Ventura, y'know, over by Laurel Canyon?"

"Yeah?"

"He wasn't paying attention, ran a red light, and smashed into Margolese's Cadillac. When the cops came, Margolese got busted because he had a person in the trunk."

"What do you mean? A live person or a dead person?"

"Alive."

"So what's the big deal?"

"He probably wasn't gonna stay that way. He was taped up in a trunk for a reason, wasn't he? Do the math. I mean, isn't this your thing, Swifty?"

"He must've saw something."

"Well, whatever it was this guy saw, or was gonna say to the cops, he got the chance. And since it was technically Jerry's fault, Margolese had him work off the jail time. You see, my whole relationship has been hijacked because he doesn't pay attention when he drives. . . . I can't go with you in here."

He walked into the stall next to hers and began to pee. Apparently the sound was helpful, because after a moment, Leroy heard a higher-pitched tinkle joining his.

Jerry was on a very different highway, riding with a thief and a mean old brown dog about a thousand miles south. An iguana blinked at the side of the road as the El Camino ripped on by. Jerry had his .38 loosely in his lap, pointed at the thief.

An hour later, they came to the lonely place in the desert where the thief and his friends had dumped Beck's body. It wasn't a spot you'd put on any tourist postcard. They parked by a large tree, the grass around it beaten down and scorched by the sun, which was blistering, beating down on the ground.

Jerry wasn't entirely sure why he was taking the trouble to retrieve Beck's body. They had only known each other a few hours, after all. But it bothered him, just leaving the kid unburied in the desert for the birds. After a morning in the sun, Beck already wasn't too nice to look at. Jerry put the thief to work, making him drag the body up from the embankment of the creek into the bed of the El Camino. Together, they covered the body with dead mesquite branches and some garbage they found, to protect it from the time being from the elements.

Once this was done, Jerry gestured the thief to sit down.

"If you're going to kill me, at least you owe me the right to know who it is that's going to send me to God," the thief said, getting more and more worried about how this was going down.

Jerry raised the .38.

"Tell me!" the thief cried, cowering.

Jerry sighed and lowered the gun.

"Listen, I'm not gonna kill you, okay? And I don't really want to do this, but I *am* gonna have to shoot you."

"But . . . why, sir? Why!"

"Because you stole from me, and you know about the pistol, and you're gonna steal again. And I don't need you coming back into this situation like a fly in the ointment."

"I won't!" the thief promised ardently. "You'll never see me again!"

Jerry shrugged. "You're getting shot. It's the middle of nowhere. It'll take you time to get to the next town, especially if you're limping. Long enough for me to do what I gotta do and go home."

"Limping!" the thief cried. "Can't you tie me up more? I mean, fuck, you shoot me? Tie me!"

"I don't have rope."

"So you *shoot* me?"

"It's the American way," Jerry assured him. He raised the gun once gain. "Where do you want it?"

The thief was truly terrified now. He was sweating. "Not in the leg," he objected. "There's arteries. I could bleed to death in mere seconds."

"The foot then. Look, the foot's pretty fair where I come from. It hurts, but it heals."

"What if you take off a fucking toe?"

Jerry walked closer and kicked the man's foot into the clear.

"Wait! Wait!" the thief cried. "Not the left!"

"Sorry." Jerry was willing to oblige, within reason. He pointed the .38 at the thief's right foot.

"On the count of three. One . . . two . . ."

The shot rang out, echoing lazily in the stillness of the desert afternoon.

Sam and Leroy sat at a booth inside the coffee shop that was part of the rest stop complex. The place was full of truckers and tourists coming and going from

Las Vegas, city of wishful thinking. Some of the people looked like they had won, most like they'd lost the family farm to one-armed bandits.

Sam nibbled on Leroy's french fries, which he had left on his plate, saying he was on a diet. He *had* managed, however, to scarf down a cheeseburger and a slice of cherry pie.

"There are a few ways to look at it," Leroy was telling her, resuming their rambling discussion. "Now, I'm not saying it doesn't make a difference. I'm saying it *does*. I'm agreeing with you. Sex is, no matter what anybody says, a very important part of a relationship. The fact that Jerry's a considerate lover says it all right there."

"You lost me," Sam admitted, whacking a ketchup bottle over Leroy's fries, coaxing the slow dribble of the condiment.

"A considerate lover. You gotta find a way to get him to expand this quality he has during sex to other areas of your relationship. Even if it only comes out in sex, it's there just the same."

"That's a good point," Sam agreed, thinking it over.

"If a person's a considerate lover, they can't be all selfish, can they, unless . . ." Sam looked curiously at Leroy, as he seemed distracted.

Leroy stubbed out the cigarette he was smoking and glanced at a man at the nearby counter who was eating a hamburger. Sam followed Leroy's gaze. The man at the counter was in his thirties, casually dressed in jeans and a baseball cap, good-looking. He met Leroy's eyes; then both of them glanced away.

"Anyway, all that stuff is internal," Leroy continued to Sam. "The point I'm trying to—"

"What was that?" Sam interrupted.

"What?"

"*That.* That moment you had."

"What moment?"

"Leroy, you checked out that guy and you had a moment. That was a moment."

"I don't know if it was a *moment*," Leroy objected.

"Are you gay?"

"As in happy?"

"As in homosexual."

"What does my sexual orientation have to do with anything that we've been talking about?"

"Nothing. It's just, I mean, something you said really bugged me back there, and now it makes sense."

"What's that?"

"I asked you if you were going to rape me and

you said, 'Not likely.' You said it so matter-of-fact, like I was repulsive and it would be ludicrous for me to think of you wanting to have sex with me."

"Well, rape is a crime of anger, not attraction," he lectured. "Second, you're not repulsive. You're quite beautiful . . . why, do you *want* me to rape you?"

"Are you gay?"

Leroy just laughed.

"I *knew* it!" she told him, triumphant.

"Do you want some kind of medal or something?" he asked, now irritated. "Some sort of trinket stating you identified a homosexual?"

"Don't be silly," she told him. She grinned. "Are you full throttle?"

Leroy laughed, despite himself. "Full throttle? Yes, I guess I am," he admitted.

"Look, I'm not trying to be a smart-ass or anything. Wow, okay, wait. This is great! This is major. I know the kind of people in your business, okay, and to me, it seems that being gay doesn't seem too conducive to the environment."

"Like I should be an interior decorator? That's insulting."

"Don't be a shit. Do you have a boyfriend?"

He shook his head. "Not at present. I have problems keeping relationships."

"Seems like everyone's having problems keeping relationships together," she assured him.

Leroy lit another cigarette, glancing at the man at the counter. As Sam watched in fascination, Leroy smiled very slightly, and the man at the counter smiled back.

Sam's grin just kept getting wider. As far as she was concerned, this was great.

A gay gangster.

Well, why not? It was an equal-opportunity world. Inexplicably, Sam felt safer somehow.

Fourteen

In a muted mood, Jerry drove back to the main highway, to the small roadside store. At least he had his wallet back, and most of his money. Things were looking up, if only slightly. Though it was hard to summon a whole lot of enthusiasm at the moment. Jerry bought two bags of chips—one for himself, the other for the dog—then he walked around to the pay phone at the side of the building. A few minutes later, he reached Ted's answering machine in Los Angeles:

"Hi, it's Ted. Leave a message. If this is my guy in need, I'm en route. Find your way to the Hotel Del Plaza. Wait for me there. Sit tight."

Jerry hung up the phone and scribbled the information on a scrap of paper in his wallet. He was starting back toward the El Camino when he heard the brown junkyard dog barking. There was a policeman standing by his car.

"*Hola*! This your dog?" the cop asked in English, smiling. He was a big man, mid-forties, with a mustache and a broad, wrinkled face. There was something about him that worried Jerry. His tan uniform was not entirely clean. And his eyes did not smile along with his mouth.

"Sort of," Jerry answered cautiously. "He's along for the ride."

"Ugly," the cop said, in admiration. "But he does have personality and that certainly counts, no?"

Jerry smiled and hoped this would be the end of it. But the cop was only getting started.

"It is your car?" he asked.

"It's a rental. I'm American."

"No shit, really!" said the cop, sarcastically. "Well, I'm Mexican."

"Cool," Jerry replied.

"You got a passport?"

Jerry reached into his back pocket and pulled out his passport, slightly banged up with travel. The cop studied it with interest, flipping pages.

"Jerry Welbach, Los Angeles, USA," he said. "Can I ask you a question, Jerry? How long have you been here in Mexico?"

"Just a little while. Few days. Pleasure."

"A few days, I see . . . I see."

It is a sad thing to lose one's liberty. A transition from a state of freedom to one in which one no longer calls the shots.

Jerry stood behind bars in the cell of the Mexican jail, not happy. There was a bad smell in the air of old vomit and urine. Worst of all, the cop had searched through the El Camino and found the antique pistol in the glove compartment. He sat behind a small cluttered desk on the opposite side of the bars, twirling the ancient and beautiful golden pistol in his hand. Jerry had just finished telling the cop about what he'd heard concerning the fable behind the pistol.

"That's not quite accurate, I'm afraid," the cop said. "The gunsmith did, indeed, craft this pistol for a prospective husband, but the story was darker, my friend."

Jerry could swear the cop's eyes twinkled.

"It's cursed, this gun. The key to this tale," said the cop, "involves the gunsmith's assistant, a poor but honorable young man in blinding love with the gunsmith's daughter . . ."

The gunsmith again walked to the center of town, his assistant walking beside him. As they approached the town square, the assistant looked over to the gunsmith's daughter, who stood at the edge of the square, watching the proceedings. When she noticed the young assistant looking at her intently, she returned his ardent gaze longingly. It was clear to anyone within sight that the two were very much in love with each other.

For months at a time, the young assistant had labored in the nearby mine, gathering the precious metals that would yield the most beautiful gun that had ever existed. With only a candle and a pick, he chipped away, day and night, until he had enough material for the gunsmith to fashion the weapon. However, the assistant soon learned that what he hoped would be a wedding gift for him was really intended for another. The gunsmith had forbidden their love. He insisted that his daughter marry the son of a nobleman.

The assistant's heart was broken, and it caused great anguish in the heart of the gunsmith's daughter. As the assistant handed the pistol to the gunsmith in the town's square, so angered was he in his bitter pain that he cursed the gun, vowing the creation would never prevail.

Now, once again, another young man was selected from the crowd to try the pistol. This one was reluctant to fire the weapon, knowing well what had happened the previous time. He shook his head in fright, pleading with the gunsmith to spare him the trial. But the nobleman was coming soon, and the gunsmith was racing against time. He had promised a pistol of unparalleled craftmanship, and with the nobleman's dowry hanging in the balance, he worked day and night to correct the pistol's problems.

The gunsmith insisted that the young man take the pistol. Another empty wine bottle was set up on a barrel twenty yards away, and the crowd instinctively stood back.

The gunsmith nodded to the poor selected youth, who shakily held up the pistol and aimed it at the bottle. Closing one eye to aim and desperately trying not to tremble, the youth desperately tried to focus. The gunsmith nodded at him again, and the young man slowly squeezed the trigger.

Bang!

As the smoke cleared, everyone opened their eyes to see that the young man was still standing. Incredulously, he checked himself over and saw that he had not been harmed by the pistol's discharge. The wine bottle had remained intact, but farther down in the square, the nose of a statue had been blown off by the stray bullet.

The young man motioned to the crowd that he was fine, as an approving roar rose up among the crowd. Suddenly, the doors of an adjacent saloon swung open, and a drunk man staggered outside, clutching his blood-soaked belly.

He weaved through the crowd, making his way to the gunsmith, at whose feet he finally fell, dead. The crowd groaned in disappointment.

Once again, the gunsmith shook his head, bent down to retrieve the pistol, and headed back to his gunshop to start all over again.

"This gun never worked properly," finished the cop, continuing to stare in awed fascination at the beautiful weapon of destruction.

"Some say that this very creation ended the poor gunsmith's life," he said, nodding grimly.

Reluctantly, the cop returned his attention to Jerry in the cell. "Well, my friend, you're free to go. But without this gun. This gun does not belong to you, or to your boss. Now it belongs to me. You understand, Mr. Jerry America?"

Jerry sighed. He understood his ass was in a sling.

The VW ripped along the Nevada highway. The little green Beetle was very crowded, now having a new passenger. Leroy drove, Sam was squeezed into the back, and Frank was in the front passenger seat. Frank was the man at the counter in the coffee shop with whom Leroy had made a definite connection.

Frank was holding up a gold mailbox key on a chain hanging around his neck. "I'm a mailman," he announced.

"Jesus Christ!" Leroy laughed.

"That's so . . . rigid," Sam told him.

"No, no, no," Frank told her. "There's a seedy underbelly to the postal service. You have no idea how many unmarked brown paper packages I deliver."

"What, porno?" Leroy asked. "Fuck off!"

"Oh, yeah! Daily, either a dirty old man, a horny housewife, or just plain old Joe Schmo, receives a small unmarked brown paper package with hours of naughty fun inside for their enjoyment. Video, blow-up dolls, dildos, pocket pussys—all that."

"Oh yeah?" Leroy asked.

"It's the Internet," Frank said. "But even with all that dirty excitement at my fingertips, every year I just have to take off. I walk out my front door and know I'm going to Vegas. I just don't know how. All I got is my wallet and an attitude. Keeps me sane. After all, guns don't kill people . . . postal workers do!"

From the backseat, Sam watched as Frank and Leroy exchanged smiles. She was strangely moved. But seeing them together made her think of Jerry, miss him, wish for a second that he was here. She quickly pushed the thought from her head. The selfish prick, of course, was probably having a great time in some swell hotel, not thinking of her at all.

Indeed, at the moment, Jerry was not thinking of Sam, but about the Mexican pistol.

He had lingered outside the Mexican jail where he had recently been incarcerated, curious as to what the cop with the mustache was going to do with the priceless pistol. He waited several hours and his patience was rewarded. He had followed the cop to a pawnshop. After the cop met the old proprietor outside, they went in to discuss business. Jerry noted the pawn shop's name, then left.

Leroy, Frank, and Sam got adjoining rooms at one of the hotels downtown, with a door that opened between them. They danced and partied in Sam's room until very late, all three of them getting reasonably pissed and extremely hilarious as the night progressed.

Sam was dressed in her jammies. It was hard to remember when she had felt quite this relaxed and silly. Finally, laughing, she collapsed onto the couch and Leroy plopped down next to her, beat. Frank was the last one on his feet. He danced over toward the adjoining room, very seductively. Sam was glad for them both. But suddenly, without warning, she felt depressed and horribly single.

Leroy followed Frank, but paused in the doorway and looked back at her.

"I'm not going anywhere," she told him.

Leroy seemed caught between two worlds. He glanced into Frank's room and then back at Sam on the couch, hesitating.

"I mean, we're in the city where I'm going to be living, remember?" She was doing her best to be bright and chirpy, but she couldn't keep up the facade. She turned away.

"What's wrong?" Leroy asked.

"You know when you're in a relationship that's going bad and you separate? And all of a sudden, everywhere you look is love and possibility? Well, that's where I'm at right now. All of Jerry's shortcomings aside, I miss him, and I'm worried about him."

"Don't worry. We'll call Nayman tomorrow, check in on everything."

Sam smiled at Leroy through her tears.

"You want me to stay?" he asked her softly.

"No, I want you to go. I *really* want you to go, Leroy!"

Leroy leaned forward as though he was going to give Sam a good night hug. But it wasn't a hug. Sam felt cold metal snap shut about her left wrist. Then Leroy attached the other end of the handcuffs to her bed, before turning to walk into the next room.

Ted had recently landed in Toluca Airport, and he was presently talking to the same car-rental representative that Jerry had dealt with. After completing the requisite paperwork, Ted was ready to roll. The car-rental rep handed Ted a set of keys and a copy of the papers he had just sighed.

"Okay, you're all set, Mr. Shurker. If you go to the front there, a shuttle will take you to your car."

Ted quickly scanned the paperwork, then folded and tucked it into his inside breast pocket. As he did, a thought struck him. "What kind of car is it, exactly?"

"It's a Chrysler, sir," replied the rep sunnily. "Brand-new."

Ted nodded unenthusiastically. "You wouldn't happen to have something a little more authentic—"

"Raoul!" The rental rep shouted out.

Ten minutes later, Ted peeled out of the lot in a souped-up candy apple–red Charger.

Fifteen

By the time Ted made his way to the Hotel Del Plaza
in Toluca, Jerry had already checked in. He was waiting for Ted outside of the hotel when he arrived.

The Hotel Del Plaza was typical vacation fare for
visiting gringos. But it was poorly constructed, a little
crumbled around the edges, like it could blow away
in the first good hurricane. Jerry wasn't complaining;
Ted had gotten them a double room to share, which
was a big improvement over his most recent situation. Outside the window, night had fallen suddenly,
as it does in the tropics. From somewhere down the
corridor, there was the sound of distant music and a
man and woman laughing. Jerry was glad there were
still a few carefree people left in the world. He was
looking forward to one night of carefree living
himself.

*　　*　　*

Jerry woke early in the morning with a headache and a dry mouth from the tequila he had drunk with Ted the night before. It took a moment to remember who and where he was: a guy with a hangover and a fucked-up mission at the Hotel Del Plaza, Mexico. Jerry raised his head and looked around. Ted's bed was empty.

Jerry was padding barefoot to the bathroom when he noticed the telephone cord on the floor disappearing beneath the bathroom door. Ted was speaking softly from the other side of the door. Jerry paused, then moved silently closer so he could hear better.

"I couldn't sleep all night," Ted was saying. "It's a third-world country here. Jerry said he saw a cockroach looked like a mayonnaise jar with legs. I think it crawled on me."

There was a pause when Jerry heard nothing. Then Ted spoke again. "Yeah, the pawnshop, he's taking me there. We're going there after breakfast. We're booked on the seven, if all goes well . . . Now, wait a minute—no, you wait a minute, Nayman! What do you gotta go and say that for? . . . Now or later? How can I misinterpret? . . . No, you didn't send the wrong guy. I'm handling things. But I never signed up for that, Bernie. I assure you, when I tell him, it'll make a difference. . . ."

The toilet flushed, cutting off the conversation. Jerry moved back away from the door. By the time Ted came out of the bathroom, Jerry was in bed, pretending to be asleep. Which wasn't easy, under the circumstances.

Later in the morning, while Ted was packing his suitcase, Jerry tried Sam's number in Los Angeles again. He got the answering machine, the same message as before, which was discouraging.

"Hi, Sam, this is like the third phone call," he told the machine. "I really wish you'd call me back here, okay? I'm getting worried."

He put down the receiver with a very gloomy feeling about life and love. Meanwhile, Ted had finished squeezing all his stuff into his suitcase and he was looking over the passports and plane tickets home, making sure everything was in order. He tossed Jerry his documents.

"I can't believe it, you know," Jerry said. "I think she really went and left to Vegas."

"I've said it before, Jerry. These women are problems, you know? You should be like me—I answer to myself, no hassles. No one rides my ass like a goddamn horse in a saddle. I'm free."

"You haven't met the right girl, Ted. You close yourself off."

"Any girl can be the right girl if the numbers work and you're willing. No way, not me! You settle, you open yourself up, you become vulnerable."

Jerry stared at him. "What's the insight into my relationship all of a sudden?"

Ted seemed uncomfortable. "Okay, look, she *is* in Vegas, Jerry," he admitted.

"You know this for a fact, huh?" Jerry glared at him. "You *knew* this all the time, didn't you?"

"Shit falls down, y'know," Ted said defensively. "Margolese called Nayman, all pissed off that you were fucking this up, told him to put someone on Sam, keep an eye. In case, you know . . ."

"I get any funny ideas?" Jerry completed the sentence, outraged. "Fuck you!"

"Come on, Jerry, don't break my balls. There's other things to consider."

"Like what, Ted? What's to consider?"

"Like, that gun is worth a lot of money, and people know you have it. She could be in fucking danger . . ."

"For fuck's sake, Ted, who is it?"

Ted sighed and shook his head, not enjoying this. "You don't know him, but it's safe to say you know *of* him. It's that fucking psycho Leroy, from Minnesota. Nayman had to do it. It was an order. Margolese would know if he didn't."

Jerry sat on the end of the bed, and laid his hands in his lap as he absorbed the news. "Wait! They're just trying to scare me," he said.

"Well, it'd do it for me," Ted assured him. "We've all heard the kidney story, Jerry. Yikes! . . . Anyway, Nayman wants us on that seven to Vegas, gun in tow. No ifs, ands, or buts. They'll meet us at the airport, and this guy Leroy, he's gonna bring the pistol to Margolese directly."

Jerry nodded slowly, wondering if Samantha was safe, and if he and Samantha were going to survive all this shit and live happily ever after. Somehow he didn't think so.

Leroy sat on the couch with his gun in his hand, watching Frank sleep on the bed. So peaceful. He held his pistol up to the morning light. A gun could be so peaceful too, very reassuring.

After a while, he stood and opened the connecting door to Sam's room. She was sleeping too. The entire world seemed at rest. Leroy went over to her and very gently unlocked the handcuffs. Then he continued into her bathroom and foraged through the little bottles of shampoo and conditioner. Not finding what he was looking for, Leroy began to rummage through Sam's toiletry, finding an extra toothbrush. Sam suddenly appeared in the doorway, watching him with a smile.

"I had to borrow. You mind?"

She shook her head and continued past him to the toilet which was behind a separate wall.

"Sleep well?" she asked while she peed, peeking her head around the dividing wall.

"Yeah. You?"

"So, who's Winston?" she asked. "The tattoo on your right arm."

Leroy grimaced, looking at his arm in the mirror. It was a small tattoo in only one color—a faded blue. All it said was WINSTON.

"He's someone I don't like very much," Leroy told her.

"You could have it removed, y'know."

Leroy nodded thoughtfully. "Maybe I will one day. C'mon," he said. "Let's get some breakfast."

Leroy and Sam walked out from the lobby door into the bright Nevada sunshine and headed down the busy street. They did not see the car parked near the front of the hotel, or the man waiting behind the wheel with a Styrofoam cup of steaming coffee in his hand, watching them.

He was a black man, expensively dressed. His eyes were hidden behind expensive sunglasses and there was a bandage on his hand where he had been recently shot. Other than that, he seemed in remarkably good shape for a person returned from the dead.

Sixteen

A waitress came over and filled Leroy's coffee cup. The waitress was in her fifties and looked like she had been a Vegas showgirl several lifetimes ago; all that remained now of her former glamour was mascara, bleached blond hair, and a voice so husky it could have pulled a sled.

When the waitress finally drifted away, Leroy continued what he had been telling Sam earlier about a recent heartbreak, a relationship that had started out like gangbusters but ultimately fizzled. Sitting there talking openly made them seem like two matrons gabbing under the dryers at a hair salon.

"At first, you're right—I thought, this guy Frank is all right," Leroy explained. "Then came no, he's *really* all right, but he doesn't feel the same way about me. Then I found out he did. But then he knew what I am, what I've done—c'mon, right? I mean, Jesus, get serious!"

"Well, what're you gonna do about it?"

"That's the thing. I didn't have to do anything. It happened absent of my will to consciously make it happen."

"Oh, really?" Sam said, cocking one eye in disbelief.

Leroy shook his head. "I was a little drunk last night. I tucked my gun up there in between the towels. And he *found* it."

"So? How'd he react?"

Leroy laughed sarcastically. "He said the past doesn't matter. He said it's the future that counts."

"Well, doesn't it?" she pressed. Sam wasn't sure, but she thought his eyes were welling up with tears.

"Leroy, life can change. People can change," she said quietly, meaningfully. "It can happen to you."

"I haven't cried in twelve years," he told her helplessly. "Don't stare. You're just making it worse. What are you, Barbara Walters?"

"It's just beautiful," she replied, truly awed.

"Let's talk about something else," Leroy blustered, turning away.

"What do you want to talk about?"

"Anything. Just . . . anything. Whatever."

Jerry, getting out of his rented El Camino,
prepares to do a little business in Mexico.

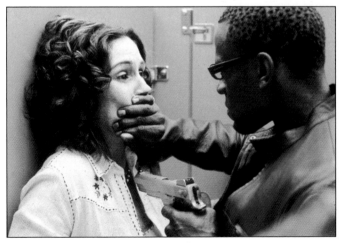

Held by a man at gunpoint, Sam is told to
remain quiet while he searches for Jerry.

Leroy waits by the car, keeping a close eye on Sam during a pit stop on their way to Vegas.

The Mexican car thief introduces Jerry to Trupillo.

Ted comes to Jerry's rescue.

The corrupt Mexican policeman reveals more of the myth surrounding the Mexican to Jerry.

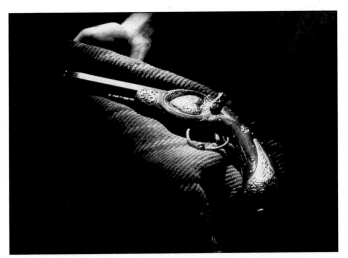

*"No one had ever laid eyes on a more beautiful gun.
Some even thought it was too beautiful to look at."*

The legendary gunsmith prepares to present
the Mexican to the nobleman in exchange for his
daughter's hand in marriage.

The fabled bride threatens to take
her life with the Mexican.

Sam, wielding the antique pistol, forces a showdown between Jerry and Nayman.

Jerry and Sam happily together again.

Brad Pitt and Julia Roberts relax between takes
during the filming of *The Mexican*.

"What was it over, the last time you cried?" she persisted. "Let's talk about that."

"Oh, that'll bring the sun right out!"

"I want to know."

He turned back to meet her gaze. "My father was sick for a long time," he said. "I got word that he was dying, taking his last breath. I waited twenty minutes for a bus to get to him, ten minutes on a subway, stuck in a tunnel . . . Then, no cabs. I ran. I fucking *sprinted*. I missed him, though, and I was so fucking pissed that I started crying."

"Shouldering an unresolved issue is difficult," Sam assured him. "Especially when it deals with a parent's impending death and there's so many things you want to say—"

"No, no," he interrupted. "I didn't have anything to say. I just wanted to see him die. See? That's how cold I am."

She stared at him. Finally, she shook her head. "I don't believe that."

"You don't know me," he said.

Sam was about to say she *did* know him. But there was a new look in Leroy's eyes as he stared back at her. The look told her not to press any further, not one step more.

* * *

Jerry and Ted walked from the hotel down a dusty dirt road to the pawnshop where Jerry had followed the cop yesterday. The road was a mess, full of children and animals and farmers selling produce from the backs of old trucks. Jaunty mariachi music was playing on a radio from inside one of the houses. Jerry thought he'd like Mexico if he was here under different circumstances, all the color and the easy, relaxed way of things down here. But on this trip, unfortunately, he had too much on his mind—like how to stay alive. He hoped like hell the antique pistol was still in the pawnshop. It wouldn't solve all his problems, but it would help.

Meanwhile, Ted was telling him gruesome tales of this psycho, Leroy, who was holding Sam hostage.

"I mean, the guy killed his *mother*—he's that fucking nuts," Ted was saying. "And you know what he did after he killed her? He cut her up and put her goddamn body parts in the freezer."

"Sure," Jerry replied skeptically.

"I swear to God, that's the story."

"Listen, if I told one guy, just one, at the next convention that *you* kept your mother cut up in the freezer for five years, you'd have a reputation too. Whether it's fact or not, makes no difference. Don't be so naive, Ted. Jesus!"

"The guy's a star," Ted insisted.

"Oh, c'mon!"

"So what are you worried about then? If he's all blowhard and bullshit?"

Jerry stopped walking. "Look, Ted, I met Leroy once, in Minnesota. It was for all of two seconds. I shook his hand and he seemed like a nice enough guy. Whether or not he lives up to this pumped-up legend of a psychotic is beside the point. What concerns me is he was hired in the first place, you see."

"Jeez, Jerry, you *really* met him?"

Ted was starting to piss Jerry off. He turned and stomped away, scattering a flock of chickens in the road. Ted hurried after him.

"Ol' Ted is not gonna let anything happen, Jerry, okay? I'm here," Ted told him in a voice that was supposed to be reassuring.

Jerry flashed him a scathing look. "Thanks, Ted. Now I feel perfectly safe."

The pawnshop was an impossible clutter of junk crowded everywhere: pots and pans, silverware, radios, wristwatches, musical instruments, sports equipment, clothes, hats, toys, car parts, you name it—all of it covered with dust and piled nearly to the ceiling in every possible square inch of space. Jerry even notice a box of old handcuffs that looked like they had been police issue over fifty years ago.

The proprietor, the lord of all this debris, was an old man with white hair who sat behind an overburdened counter at the rear of the store, wearing a philosophical expression on his face.

"*Hola*," he said cautiously, watching the gringos approach.

Ted pulled out his gun. It was a big, fat .45 and he promptly stuck it in the old man's face.

"I-no-fuck-around," Ted told him. "You-*comprendez*? Gun-gun-loaded-BANG-dead."

The old man studied Ted impassively. "Do you have a speech impediment, or are you under the impression that I don't speak English?" he inquired.

"Gimme the fucking gun," Ted demanded. "The pistol."

"What pistol?"

"You know what I'm talking about. Let's go. Chop-chop."

Jerry tried a kinder, more gentle approach. "Look, what's your name?" he asked the old man.

"Joe."

Jerry smiled with encouragement. "Look, Joe, do like he says," Jerry suggested. "We'll be out of here before you know it. Okay?"

Joe glanced from one gringo to the other. Finally, with a disdainful sigh, he nodded and led Jerry into a back room. Ted kept watch by the counter, awed by all the junk everywhere. He was picking out a pair of ancient handcuffs from the box, thinking they might be useful, when Jerry returned carrying a dirty canvas bag.

"You got it?"

"I got it," Jerry told him.

"Okay. Just have a seat, amigo," Ted said to the old man. "I gotta make sure you don't go anywhere for a while. Nothing personal, you understand."

Joe shrugged fatalistically and sat down on the floor where Ted had indicated. Ted knelt next to him and handcuffed the old man to an iron grate on the floor. He was just finishing up when he felt something cold and hard pressed against the back of his head. He turned to see Jerry pointing his .38 revolver at him.

Ted's expression went through several phases of shock and disbelief.

"Jerry, have you lost your mind?" he cried, freaked out.

"I heard you this morning," Jerry told him. "When you were in the bathroom."

"Well, so what? A guy's gotta pee. Jerry, for Christ's sake. . . ."

"What were you guys talking about on the phone, Ted? Come on, deny it."

"Put the gun away."

"What?" Jerry insisted. "To off me? Is that what was discussed? To *off* me?"

"Jerry, I would never—"

"Come on, Ted, deny it."

Ted tried to squirm out of it. He sighed, he shook his head, and then he stared up at Jerry in helpless misery. But, finally, he nodded.

"Okay, Jerry," he admitted, "that's what he said."

"So you were lying to me when you told me I would walk away from this?"

"No, that's what he said."

Jerry considered the conflicting information. "So you're lying now about him asking to off me? Which is it?"

"No, Nayman told me to do it, but . . ."

"But that's your portion, Ted. Right?"

"No!"

"Isn't that how it goes?" Jerry persisted. "Seventeen portions left to Boca, right?"

"Jerry, I wouldn't do that portion," he swore, very sincerely. "I swear. I swear, Jerry. C'mon."

Jerry studied him hard. "One hand, they tell you to bring me in. The other, to take me out. Why're you being told to do two contradicting things? You don't ask a question?"

Ted's face grew slack. Indeed, he had been given two very different directives from Nayman. "I just . . . I don't know."

"I mean, isn't that weird?"

"Yeah, it's weird."

"Something's going on, right? What is it?"

"I don't know," Ted repeated, unhappily.

"What's going on, Ted? What's the truth here? The *truth*?"

But Ted could only shake his head, bewildered. As a guy just doing his portion, he had never tried looking at the whole picture before.

"Exactly," Jerry told him. "You don't know. Because you're just doing your fucking part. I'm not going down because you don't know. You see my predicament, Ted?"

Ted nodded, seeing the predicament. There was no refuting logic.

"You're my guy, Ted," Jerry told him, tossing him a pair of handcuffs from the box.

"You're my guy, Jerry," Ted agreed, weakly. Weighing confusing directives against friendship, Ted knew that Jerry was right. He couldn't do his portion without knowing why. Ted walked over beside Joe and sat down, extending his hands around the iron gate.

Jerry handcuffed Ted next to Joe; then he left the pawnshop with the dirty canvas bag, turning the sign on the front door from ABIERTO to CERRADO.

A group of children watched him stride confidently from the store across the dirt road, a renewed purpose to his step.

Jerry smiled and pointed his finger like a gun at them: *Bang!*

Frank woke up alone in the double bed he had shared last night with Leroy. The air-conditioning hummed and the smell of old cigarette smoke hung in the air. The connecting door to Sam's room was open, but neither Sam nor Leroy was anywhere around. Frank imagined they'd probably gone out for breakfast.

Frank got up leisurely, turning on the radio to listen to some tunes. He found a cigarette on the side table and wandered into Sam's room in his underwear in search of a light. The ashtrays were full and there were glasses and an empty vodka bottle on the coffee table, reminding him why he felt such a dull ache in his head.

He returned to his own room and headed for the

shower, hoping that steam and hot water would transform him back into a human being again. Before he entered the bathroom, he didn't bother to lock the hotel room door. As he started the shower, the hotel room door was manipulated open. Just as Frank stepped into the shower, a well-dressed black man, gun drawn, inched his way across the room toward the bathroom.

Seventeen

Samantha and Leroy walked in silence back to the hotel. Sam had heard people say that Las Vegas was the same day or night, a city that ran on its own schedule twenty-four hours a day, nonstop, outside of the regular march of time. But there *was* a difference, she thought. At night, Vegas sparkled with a billion kilowatts of light, lending the city an aura of sheer magic. But by day, everything looked a little shabby, revealed too clearly in the bright desert sun.

Sam was surprised to see that a crowd had gathered in the parking lot of their hotel. As they drew near, they began to hear snippets of conversation from the onlookers.

"What happened out here?" someone asked an elderly woman.

"Somebody killed themself. Swan dive, right off the balcony," the woman said matter-of-factly, as if it were a regular occurrence in Vegas.

"C'mon," Leroy told her, taking hold of her arm and leading her into the hotel.

They walked quickly through the lobby, toward the bank of elevators, bypassing the slot machines that blinked and beckoned. When they got off the elevator at their floor, Sam was surprised to see several uniformed hotel security people knocking door to door, communicating to associates downstairs on their walkie-talkies. A nagging worry was starting to eat at Sam and she could tell from Leroy's face that he was worried too.

Leroy opened Sam's door and led the way inside. The radio was still playing from the adjoining room, the door half-open.

Sam followed Leroy into the next room. The glass door to the outside balcony was open, the white curtains wafting in the wind. The moment Leroy saw the curtains, he stopped in his tracks, breathless, as if he had been hit in the stomach. He was experienced enough to know what had happened.

"No," Sam told him. "It's just not possible. Not Frank . . ."

Leroy turned slowly to face her. The expression in

his eyes was terrible, vacant, like a man destroyed. Seeing it, Sam knew that it was Frank who had hit the pavement below. Her face trembling, she began to cry. Suddenly there was a knock on the outside door and Leroy got a grip on himself. He put his finger to his mouth, shushing her. The knock resounded again, louder. Leroy made a motion for her to freeze and just stay put; then he walked through Sam's room and opened up the door. She leaned against the wall, starting to cry softly, uncertain her unsteady legs would hold her as she listened to Leroy deal with the security man outside in the hallway.

"Hello, sir, I'm sorry to intrude, but I'm afraid there's been a terrible incident," the security man said. "May I ask, are all parties in your room accounted for?"

"Yes . . . just my wife and I," Leroy answered. Looking around, he saw that similar conversations were being held between security guards and guests in and down the corridors. Frank's room would be next.

"Okay, sir. Thank you very much. I'm sorry to have disturbed you."

"No problem at all. What happened? Everything all right?"

After the security guard left, Leroy came back into the next room, where Sam was leaning against the wall, still sobbing. His face was set—hard and unreadable.

"Pack your things," he told her gruffly.

Sam was like a zombie. She couldn't find the strength move.

"Do it!" he ordered. His harsh tone set her in motion. She went to her room to pack. Alone, Leroy sat down in a chair facing the open window, the curtains fluttering in the breeze. He let his face collapse. He was staring at the floor when he noticed something glittering on the carpet near his foot. It was Frank's gold mailbox key, on a golden chain. Leroy leaned over and picked it up carefully. The chain was broken, the soft metal ripped apart. Leroy shook his head and sighed hard, trying to rein back his emotion. Emotion was shit on any job, he knew, and it wouldn't help in this situation, and certainly it wouldn't bring Frank back. At last, almost guiltily, he slipped the gold key and chain into his pocket, a keepsake of something good that might have developed in a different kind of world than the one in which he lived.

Leroy fished in his pocket for a cigarette and a book of hotel matches. He lit the cigarette and was dropping the dead match into an ashtray on the bedside table when something in the ashtray caught his eye. He blew out a stream of smoke and picked up the ashtray, studying it more closely.

It was a curious thing. There were a number of butts squashed out—the pile of ashes was pretty disgusting, really—and almost all of the smoked cigarettes had white filters, the Pall Malls that he and Frank had been smoking last night. But one didn't match.

There was a single butt with an orange filter that definitely did not belong.

Sam stood in front of the sink in her bathroom, patting her eyes with cold water. She couldn't stop crying. Emotionally speaking, she was a mess. Physically speaking too. She was wishing Jerry was there, dabbing her face gently with the towel and speaking soothing words to her, when the bathroom door opened.

Sam turned, thinking it was Leroy. But it wasn't Leroy; it was a ghost. It took Sam a few seconds to get her eyes and her brain in sync, because what she saw was blatantly impossible: it was the well-dressed black man with the designer sunglasses she had last seen lying dead in the ladies' room in the shopping mall somewhere in the California/Nevada desert. And just like before, the ghost was pointing a gun at her. Sam's eyes went wide with terror but he put his hand over her mouth before she could scream.

"Shh!" he whispered, placing the cold barrel of his pistol up to her forehead.

Sam didn't understand any of this, except for the fact that this elegantly dressed apparition from the dead was going to kill her if she didn't do everything he wanted. She nodded, trying to indicate how well she was going to behave herself.

He pulled her from the bathroom, then walked her slowly to the adjoining room, holding his gun to her left ear. He gestured for her to stop when they reached the open door. Very carefully, he peeked over her shoulder into the next room. His eyes darted from one side of the room to the other, then stopped, staring at the bedside table. Sam saw what he saw: a recently lit cigarette burning in the ashtray.

Sam couldn't imagine where Leroy had gone, but she hoped he hadn't gone far. Meanwhile, the black man was very slowly turning his head, scanning the interior of the hotel bedroom. She followed his gaze to the adjoining room, which was standing curiously wide open. Sam had a kind of déjà vu feeling that she couldn't immediately identify. Then she suddenly remembered that the bathroom door was open exactly like the door of the rest room in the mall, the first time she and Leroy and the black man had lived through this strangely recurrent scene. The black man was smiling; he had picked up on the similarity immediately, and this time it looked like he wasn't going to be fooled.

Sam was trying desperately to think of some way to warn Leroy. But the man seemed to sense her intentions; he pressed the barrel of his gun hard against her head and made her sit down on the floor. She was helpless. She watched as he crept soundlessly across the carpet, closer to the open door. Then suddenly, he began firing at the door itself, unloading his entire clip into it. The noise was terrible in the enclosed room, as the sound of gunfire and splintering wood ricocheted violently off the walls. When he was satisfied no one could be alive behind the door, the black man reached and ripped it back.

But there was no one there.

No Leroy. Nothing. The man was obviously confused. Somehow he had misread the situation.

From the opposite end of the room, Leroy poked his head out from behind the blowing white curtains.

"You dumb motherfucker," he said calmly.

The black man spun around, but he never had a

chance. Leroy began firing, shot after shot, sending the man sprawling back hard against the wall, knocking him down to the floor. The black man was hit repeatedly, his gun tumbled from his hand onto the carpet. Yet he wouldn't die. It was monstrous. Sam watched in horror as he sat up and tried to reach for his gun. He almost had the weapon in his grasp when Leroy blasted him again, blowing him onto his back. He lay gasping in pain, yet still he wouldn't quit. He was struggling to sit up again when Leroy fired another shot. Each bullet was like a mule kick in the stomach, but the black man seemed to possess superhuman stamina.

At last, Leroy stood directly over the man, pointing his gun in his face.

"You're a well-dressed one. I'll give you that. But still a dumb motherfucker," Leroy told him. "Wearin' Kevlar, huh?"

"Leroy, don't," Sam told him breathlessly. "Please don't do it!"

The black man started to gurgle something, but it was incoherent. Kevlar or not, he had taken a beating.

"You think I should listen to her?" Leroy said, never taking his eyes off the man on the floor. "Yeah? Well, wanna know what I think?"

Leroy held his hand to his ear, waiting for a reply. But the man on the floor could only burble pitifully.

"Kevlar is for pussies," Leroy whispered. "And *this* is for Frank!"

Leroy pointed the barrel at the black man's head and pulled the trigger.

Eighteen

Jerry drove to the Toluca Airport and turned in his rented El Camino with a feeling of satisfaction. Despite the many obstacles, here he was, still alive, with the precious pistol back in his possession. He had kept his part of the bargain, and with a little luck, Old Man Margolese would understand that his grandson's death was an accident and take a kindly view of Jerry's hard-won efforts.

At heart, Jerry realized, he was still an optimist.

He carried his sling bag through the busy terminal and ducked into the men's room. He kept having second thoughts about where to stash the old gun for the flight to Las Vegas, whether to keep it on him or check it through with his bag. The pistol had caused him too much grief already, coming and going, what with car thieves and dirty cops. His instinct was to keep the gun close to his body, but he wasn't sure if maybe an old flintlock pistol would cause problems with security. In the end, he thought it safer to check it through.

Jerry locked himself into a stall, set his bag down on the toilet seat, and took the antique pistol out from the dirty canvas. He held the gun for a moment, staring at it appreciatively, the gold and silver and polished wood gleaming under the rest room's fluorescent lights. He almost had to force himself to tear his eyes away, wrap the gun carefully in one of his shirts, and stuff it inside his bag, out of sight. He hoped he was making the right choice.

He left the bathroom and made his way through the crowded airport to the AeroMexico ticket counter. There was a long line of returning gringos ahead of him, single party types and honeymoon couples. They all looked like they were coming down from too much fiestaing and way too little sleep. The ticket agent behind the counter was an attractive, dark-haired woman, with a pleasant enough smile, but she seemed almost sadistically pleased to keep people waiting. The line trickled forward in slow motion.

Jerry eventually arrived at the counter. The dark-haired attendant took his old return ticket and started typing efficiently into her computer. Meanwhile, it seemed to Jerry that the guy who was behind him in line was standing a little too close to his bag. Probably he was being paranoid, but the jinxed pistol had caused everything to go wrong, and he wasn't willing to take any chances. He picked up the bag defensively and put it on the scale, keeping his eye peeled. This was the home stretch, after all. In a few hours he and the beautiful gun would be in Las Vegas. . . .

Jerry was dreaming a little, getting ahead of himself, wondering if Samantha was going to be glad to see him.

The ticket agent put a tag on his bag and he watched nervously as she set it on the moving conveyer belt.

"My bag'll make the flight?"

"They'll run it down there. I'll just need to see your passport."

Jerry reached into his jacket pocket and handed her his passport. She thumbed it open, looked at his photo and then at him.

"Oh, I'm afraid there's a mistake," she said, handing back the passport.

Jerry was ready to explode. "No? No!" *A mistake?* But he looked at the passport and nearly gagged.

Instead of *his* photo on the main page, there was a fine color portrait of Ted Shurker staring at him with a vaguely shit-eating grin. Jerry saw what he had done. Somehow he had taken the wrong passport back in the hotel room this morning.

She slowly tore Jerry's ticket up into small, deliberate pieces.

Late at night in Los Angeles, Bobby Victory was still in his office at Margolese Holdings, Inc., going over the accounts. Bobby was no slouch. He was ambitious, a young guy with a future, which was why he was working late.

He heard a phone ring in Bernie Nayman's office next door. It seemed odd, a call coming this time of night. After a moment, Bobby got curious and strolled into the next office to see a fax coming in on Nayman's machine. It was a single page and Bobby decided, what the hell, he might as well give it a read. In the business he was in, information was gold.

"Son of a bitch!" he cried.

At first he was angry. Really pissed. But then he considered the matter on a deeper level and a smile touched the corner of his lips. He made himself comfortable at Nayman's desk with the sheet of paper in hand, wondering, as he was apt to do, how best to advance the career goals of Bobby Victory.

So there he was. *Nowhere.* Still in Toluca, Mexico, when he should have been on a jet to Las Vegas, U.S.A.

He watched the plane leave without him; then he made his way back across the terminal to the rental-car company. By now Jerry was feeling extremely stressed. Anger and frustration had given him simultaneous heartburn and headache. A guy couldn't take much more. To make it worse, he started thinking about Samantha in Las Vegas, missing her so badly it nearly took his breath away.

For Sam's sake, Jerry stopped and tried to visualize something good, anything at all. It wasn't easy, but after some heavy meditative moments had passed, he saw that there were a few things he could count as blessings. Two things, to be precise: his old El Camino was still available from the rental company, and at the very last moment, the luggage handlers had been able to stop his bag from going to Las Vegas without him.

He still had the pistol. Now he only had to figure out how to get the beautiful Mexican gun out of the country. It was almost like the gun had a will of its own and refused to leave.

*   *   *

Moonlight seeped in through the front window of the cluttered, musty pawnshop where Ted and Joe, the old proprietor, were handcuffed to the iron grate, less than a foot apart. It was now four in the morning, and they had experienced several hours of intense togetherness, captive audience to one another. Frankly, Ted couldn't believe the nerve of the old man: Joe had been trying to *blackmail* him, for Christ's sake, with the wildest bunch of bullshit Ted had ever heard!

"I'm starving," Ted moaned, visualizing a roast beef hero with pickles, onions, swiss cheese, tomato, lettuce, jalapeño peppers, and extra mayo and mustard.

"Let's get back to what we were talking about," Joe suggested. "It'll pass the time."

Ted rolled his eyes. "Oh, boy!" he said. "Yeah, let's get back to that for a second, sure. Do you know the extent of what you're asking me to do here? Marriage is a big, big thing. And besides, we're talking about something that didn't belong to you in the first place."

"Look," Joe said reasonably, "that cop, he paid me a twelve thousand deposit to fence it for him, which I'll have to return, making me twelve thousand in the hole."

"You're wrong, Joe, you're wrong."

"More even, if you take into account the full amount of the fence commission, which is . . . I don't even want to think about it. That was my life, that deal."

Ted nodded, trying to be fair. "I hear what you're saying," he replied, "but that is not, and never was, your money. That dirty cop stole the gun from Jerry, who was giving it to my boss, the rightful owner, you see?"

"Regardless, when my daughter arrives and sees her poor daddy, I'll instruct her to get the keys and let me out. And I'll have no other alternative than to call the policeman and tell him of this misfortune."

Ted considered this. The idea of the cop coming back into the picture was shitty news, all around. And so was the old man's alternative proposal: Ted would marry his daughter and take her to live in the United States, and these things being accomplished, Joe would *never* deal with a dirty cop to the detriment of his future son-in-law. It was blackmail of the cruelest, most shocking degree.

"Your English is pretty goddamn good, y'know, Joe," Ted said meditatively. "Listen, I never considered getting married in the U.S.A., let alone Mexico. I'm a difficult man to live with, stuck in my ways.

The fact you want your daughter to lead a fruitful life in the States, Joe, that's just got nothin' to do with me."

"She's healthy and strong," Joe told him. "A childbearer."

"I bet," Ted sighed.

Nineteen

Leroy and Sam stood together at the arrivals terminal in the Las Vegas airport, watching the passengers who had just arrived from Toluca, Mexico, coming out through customs. One by one the travelers departed with their bags in tow, some on little suitcase wheels, others piled high on airport carts. It was a holiday crowd with bright shirts and suntans. Some of them were greeted by friends and family; others made their own way alone out of the building into the hot afternoon. But not one of them was Jerry Welbach.

As Sam watched the passengers file past, her emotions were like the *Titanic*, going down to the deepest depths of the sea. It surprised her because she hadn't admitted to herself how much she had been looking forward to seeing Jerry. She began to sniffle, and the sniffle turned into a sob, and soon she was outright bawling.

"Where's Jerry?" Sam cried.

"You remember when I said, at the beginning, that if everything doesn't get all funky, things would be cool?" Leroy asked.

Bernie Nayman urgently needed to resolve a slight problem-in-progress with his colleague, Bobby Victory, who was seated at this very moment on the other side of Nayman's desk. It was a tricky situation because Bobby had picked up a fax on Bernie's machine that was supposed to be for Bernie's eyes only. A very *sensitive* fax, as it happened. And now the arrogant little prick had this sensitive piece of paper in his hand, waiting for an explanation.

Nayman considered two options. The first was reaching into his upper right-hand drawer, where he kept a 9mm semiautomatic, and blasting the smug smile off Bobby's face forever. The second was being nice, working out their differences in a mature manner. Bernie took the second approach only because he wasn't entirely certain he could get away with the first.

"So, what's up?" Bobby pressed, still grinning.

"You're right," Nayman told him, doing his best imitation of sincerity. "It *is* an offer for the gun. Yeah, I can see how this looks, but I've just been trying to get some better numbers together."

Bobby nodded, not buying it. A hint of malice crept into his smile.

"You have no intention of giving that gun to Margolese, do you, Bernie?"

Nayman shrugged and raised the palms of his hands in surrender. He was busted—he knew it.

"Look, Bobby. I know you're loyal, and that's good. Nobody's debating that. But, if you hear me out, maybe I can shed a little light on what happens when there's too much loyalty. When the person who's supplying the loyalty crosses a line and becomes an A-hole."

Bobby cocked his head thoughtfully to one side to show how deeply he was listening.

Nayman continued, starting to feel a small wave of encouragement: "Lemme ask you, in your skulking around, going through private things in other people's offices, did you manage to discover that he's shutting us down?"

"Shutting us *down*?" Bobby repeated.

"That's right. You, me, everybody."

"I don't understand," Bobby admitted, now thoroughly perplexed.

Nayman smiled sarcastically. "What do you mean? What, you didn't get the memo? The severance package, the bonus? No?"

Bobby shook his head. "No. Nothing."

Nayman leveled his gaze meaningfully, his point made. "Neither did I," he said. "The difference between you and me is that I know when I'm being fucked and you don't. Because you're standing on the wrong fucking line."

Bobby seemed crestfallen. The arrogant little schmuck wasn't nearly as bright as he thought he was, Nayman thought.

"Go on, Bobby. Take another look at that number. Take a *good* look," Nayman urged.

Bobby studied the fax in his hand. "It's a lot of money," he said.

"You bet it's a lot of money!" Nayman agreed. "I know for a fact that they offered that to Margolese, and he turned them down, cold. *Cold,* can you imagine? Kind've makes you wonder what he's getting . . . what *his* package is."

While Bobby was digesting all this, Nayman took a pen from his desk and wrote a number on a pad of paper: $10,000. He handed the pad to Bobby, who studied it with profound interest.

"Let me help you get back in the right line, and do for you what he should have done, Bobby," Nayman said persuasively.

Just then, Estelle, the office secretary, buzzed Nayman's office a second time, interrupting. "He's still holding," she said. "What do you want me to tell him?"

Nayman looked hard at Bobby.

"Can I count on your cooperation?" he asked.

Standing at a pay phone near a gift shop in the Las Vegas airport, Leroy was starting to get slightly pissed off. Estelle had kept him on hold for nearly ten minutes now. He came to attention as Bobby Victory came on the line.

"Yeah, Bobby, still here," he suddenly said. He listened carefully and began writing in a small spiral notebook. "Right," he said after a while. "That's their hotel?" He listened some more. He said, "Yeah, okay, fine," then hung up the phone.

Sam looked at him. "What?" she asked.

Leroy glanced at his watch. "Okay, Plan B is now in effect."

"Plan B?" she repeated sarcastically.

He smiled. "I hope you don't get airsick."

Twenty

A rosy dawn touched the dirty windows of the Mexican pawnshop, and soon morning itself blossomed outside the building, full of heat and noise and dust.

It had been a very long night for Ted and Joe, the white-haired proprietor, handcuffed to the floor less than a foot apart. When morning broke, Joe was still working on his crazy scheme of getting his daughter into the U.S.A., and to a life of fabulous wealth north of the border.

"It's more complex," Ted objected, trying to explain matters to Joe. "There's green card meetings, background searches. They're not stupid, y'know. Besides, I got a mother too, a mother I've done nothing but disappoint. I'm Jewish by religion, y'know."

"You said you thought about settling—"

"I've *thought*, exactly! But, Joe, the thought of living my life running pawnshops is a whole other thing."

"Not just pawnshops, Ted. The best damn pawnshops in America, coast to coast!"

Ted heard the front door open. He strained his neck, and from feet up, he saw a very beautiful young woman walk into the store. She was sultry, dark-haired, voluptuous, a goddess in her early twenties.

"That's . . . that's . . ." He couldn't entirely speak.

"That's Emmanuelle," Joe told him proudly. "My daughter."

She swayed a little as she walked, coming over to where her father and the gringo sat. Her lovely brow was creased, showing concern. But when she saw they were okay, the crease went away and she smiled. Her smile was like the sun coming out through storm clouds. Like a rainbow.

"We were robbed," Joe explained. "This is Ted."

"Where's the key to the cuffs?"

"In the lockbox," her father told her.

"Where's the key to the lockbox?"

"I got the key," Ted assured her.

She turned and looked at him with her dazzling smile. "To the cuffs or the lockbox?" she asked.

"To America," he replied, staring right into her

dark, beautiful eyes. Joe leaned over and gleefully kissed Ted on the cheek.

An hour later, Jerry Welbach peered through the dusty window from the street into the cluttered pawnshop. He was disappointed to find no sign of either Ted or the old man he had left handcuffed on the floor. They had simply vanished. He tried the door, hoping to get inside to investigate the matter further. But the door was locked.

He turned and began walking to his El Camino, baffled and discouraged. He had been hoping to get his passport the easy way from Ted; now it appeared he was going to have to go through the whole riga-marole with the U.S. Consulate. He had already left two messages with the consulate earlier this morning, but the person he needed to speak to wasn't there. Jerry was unlocking the El Camino when he heard a familiar bark. It was the old brown junkyard dog he thought he had left behind as a distant memory. The dog was sitting on the road, drooling and slobbering over the same deflated football. While Jerry watched, the animal surprised him by jumping into the back of the El Camino. It was heartwarming to have such a loyal, if mangy, friend.

Jerry drove back to the Hotel Del Plaza and parked

in the lot, leaving the dog in the back of the truck. He went into the lobby, passing a number of potted plants and atmospheric Mexican chairs of heavy, beaten wood that had probably been turned out by the factory load for tourist hotels. The clerk behind the reception desk was a slight, welcoming young man in a flowery shirt and white pants. His teeth sparkled when he smiled.

"*Hola*, Señor Welbach," the clerk said pleasantly.

"Hi, I was wondering if the U.S. Consulate has called back."

"No, sir. Not yet."

"Well, it's kind've important. I lost my passport, so if . . ."

The clerk nodded with understanding and waved Jerry closer. He gestured to an older man sitting across the lobby, who was trying to make sense out of a Mexican newspaper that he had spread in front of him.

"That's Señor Williamson," the clerk said discretely. "He's been waiting for that very same call."

"Oh, really? The whole morning?"

"Since March, señor!"

Jerry began to laugh hysterically. Just at that moment, the phone rang and the clerk picked up.

"Hotel Del Plaza? Yes, as a matter of fact he's right here. Hold, please . . . Señor, it's for you."

The clerk handed the phone to a still snickering Jerry, who snatched it away and eagerly put the receiver to his ear.

"Hello?" Jerry said. He was about to launch into the particulars of his lost passport when he realized this was not the U.S. Consulate.

"You bastard!" cried a familiar voice. " '*Hello?*' he says, like 'Hello, everything is fine, my life is great'?"

Jerry tried to get a word in, but Sam was just winding up and would not let him speak.

"I thought you could be dead!" she cried. "I've been worried sick! And you answer the phone 'Hello' like you're confirming a room service order!"

For Jerry, this was all very confusing, to have Sam yelling at him out of nowhere. "Sam? Sam!" He was doing his best to get a basic reality check on the situation when he heard the phone on the other end dropping and hitting the ground. He heard a man's voice in the background arguing with Sam, telling her to take the receiver. Finally, she was on the phone once more.

"Baby, where are you?" Jerry asked.

"You mean, like, are we talking cosmically? Because if that's what you mean, you didn't really care about that, did you? If you mean geographically, well, that's another issue, isn't it? And I don't know if I want to tell you."

Jerry heard the man's voice again. *"Ask about the gun,"* the man hissed in an ominous undertone.

"Is that Leroy?" Jerry asked, concerned. "Did he touch you?"

"Do you have any idea what I've been through the last few days?" Sam demanded to know.

"Sam," he told her, "whatever you've been through, multiply it by a thousand times and you'll begin to understand where I'm at."

"Oh, there you go! It's a competition. Tit for tat, tat for tit."

"Stop yelling at me! For Christ's sake! Are you okay? Where are you?"

"Toluca Airport!" she shouted. "Things are shitty, Jerry. Really shitty."

Before Jerry could ask why things were shitty, he heard the man's voice again in the background: "Tell him he shows with the gun, nothing'll happen to you."

Now Sam was speaking to Leroy. "He doesn't care about that. He only cares about himself, you know. It's the same old thing with him."

Jerry interrupted. "What're you . . . Why are you airing personal things with complete strangers?"

At least he got her attention back. "You know what, Jerry? I don't think you classify someone who you just perpetrated a killing with a complete fucking stranger. . . ."

She was crying now, really bawling. But she still wouldn't let Jerry get a word in.

". . . Thanks to you, Jerry Welbach, the police have my Kotex card, my credit pads, and who knows what else!"

Jerry rubbed his eyes in frustration. She was really a mess.

"Sam, what did you say?" Jerry asked.

But Leroy had taken the phone. "Just settle down, Jerry," he advised.

"What's wrong with her? What did you do to her?" Jerry demanded.

"Jerry, settle down," Leroy repeated. "We had a slight situation, but it should occur to you, I'm a professional and I know what I'm doing. Now, let's all chill a minute here. First off, what happened? Did you get lost?"

"Yeah, I got lost, five years ago," Jerry muttered.

Leroy missed this observation, due to a flight announcement on his end. "Are you there? I couldn't hear you."

"I'm here. Forget it, nothing," Jerry told him dismally.

"Nothing? I hope you have *something!*"

"Make sure you return her with all ten toes. You hear me?" Jerry warned.

"I understand. Just come down here, pick us up, and we'll square things away. You got a special woman here, Jerry. We all know how you can get, so let's not have any of that business." Leroy paused, then added, significantly: "This is a time of selflessness."

Jerry couldn't believe his ears. *Selflessness!* He was about to respond strongly about this particular issue, but that wasn't possible.

Leroy had hung up on him.

Twenty-one

Samantha and Leroy sat next to each other on the curb outside the Toluca airport, waiting for Jerry to show. Sam watched hotel vans and taxis come and go, some of them very beat up. The air was warm and fragrant, more exotic than U.S.A. air. At another time, she might have found it romantic to be in such a foreign place, but not today. Even Leroy seemed out of spirits.

"I want to ask you a question, and it's a tough one," Leroy said to Sam. "So think about it for a while before you answer. In your situation, which, granted, is pretty hard to come by, you have two people who really, truly, love each other, but just can't get it together. When do you get to that point of enough is enough?"

Sam listened, studying her feet. "See, you know

exactly where I'm at, Leroy. But I *have* been thinking about it, and, sadly, I have that answer."

"You should let it cook," he told her. "Think on it."

"No, no, you *know* when it's over. When . . . Okay, I have it—whatever psychosomatic manifestations are . . ." She stopped and changed tracks, in typical Samantha fashion, trying to best express her thoughts to Leroy. "Here's the thing about me. I happen to be a product of my emotions, versus being a product of my environment, like him. Which he is, exactly. I mean, he's . . . For me, I need sunshine to grow, okay? It's like a projection, y'know. I have goals. That's who I am."

Leroy stared a her, considering her semicoherent spiel. It was a tribute to his sensitivity that he understood, more or less, what she had just said.

"That's your answer? That's not right. There's a right answer here, but that's not it," he told her. He paused, just so that what he had said would sink in. But when he started to speak again, he got choked up and looked away.

"Look, in my business I'm surrounded by loneliness, finality. No matter what your take is on an afterlife, it's scary and people leave it alone. Usually, the ones that I send off that have experienced love . . .

the ones that gave of piece of themselves to someone and tried to make a go in this shit life—they're a little less scared. A little knowing smile in their eyes, behind the fear of the unknown, the knowledge that someone, somewhere, loves them and will miss them. I see it from time to time and I am awed by it. Maybe I wouldn't be saying this if it wasn't for Frank, but the question is sort of loaded. I said, when two people love each other, totally, truthfully, all the way. The answer to the question is simple to me in your case: it's never. *Never*."

Samantha thought about what he had said. She didn't know how to reply. Leroy had a good point, but she still wasn't sure how it was going to work out between herself and Jerry.

Sam and Leroy sat waiting in the sun. After a while, Leroy sighed and opened up his suitcase. He foraged around discreetly in his underwear and pulled out his handgun.

"Let's just hope Jerry's not stupid," he said, tucking the gun down into his waistband.

Back at the Hotel Del Plaza parking lot, Jerry was also stuffing a gun into his waistband, transferring his snub-nosed .38 revolver from his luggage to where he could get to it quickly. Once he had his modern weapon stowed away, he took a moment to consider what to do the antique Mexican pistol. On impulse, he took it from his bag and slipped it into the glove compartment of the El Camino. He liked the idea of having both guns very close at hand, in case the upcoming situation became fluid.

Now there was only one more small matter to take care of. Before setting out, he walked around to the bed of the truck, where the junkyard dog was sleeping, his deflated football not far from his slathering jaws. Jerry lowered the tailgate.

"Out!" he ordered. Jerry was more than pissed; his tone was deadly. His voice must have carried conviction, because the dog stirred, sat uncertainly, and for the first time ever, did exactly as Jerry said, slinking out of the back of the El Camino onto the ground.

Twenty minutes later, Jerry—not even waiting for one stoplight to turn green and running the red light—drove up a ramp at the Toluca Airport that said ARRIVALS in Spanish and English, dodging several minivan taxis who changed lanes psychotically. The normal traffic rules didn't seem to apply in Mexico.

He saw Samantha before she saw him: sitting kind of slouchy and sexy on the curb. It was a pose he recognized, her chin propped up meditatively on one hand. She looked good, a sight for sore eyes. Jerry felt aglow just looking at her, like some knot inside his chest had just loosened with relief. There was a man sitting next to her. He was a hefty man, prematurely balding, wearing a little goatee on his chin. He didn't look overtly dangerous, but Jerry suspected otherwise. The knot in his chest tightened again: there were going to be some tricky moments ahead.

He pulled the El Camino over to the curb and watched Sam's face as she spotted him. At first her face seemed to light up, but only for an instant. It was immediately replaced by a smoldering glower. He was still on her shit list. Jerry sighed, then pushed open the passenger door for them, leaning over from the inside of the cab. He shifted his attention to the dangerous element here: the man with the goatee.

Leroy nodded, studying him. Jerry saw he had a gun shoved down into the front of his pants, just as Jerry did. Which didn't make this a fabulously warm and friendly occasion. Leroy threw both his and Samantha's bags into the back of the truck and then he slid into the front seat next to Jerry. Sam got in next to the door, as far from Jerry as the cab would allow. She avoided looking at him. Jerry pulled out into the traffic, the El Camino accelerating with a deep macho rumble.

"This is a *funky* rental," Leroy observed. He smiled pleasantly. "Well, well, here we are."

Neither Sam nor Jerry said a word. Jerry stared straight ahead, minding the traffic, and Sam gazed hypnotically out her window. It was a thick silence, loaded with unsaid accusations, and with every mile that went by, the stress level in the cab seemed to go up another few notches.

"Look," Leroy said finally. "We're all a little grouchy right now. We'll get something to eat, get the gun, and we'll all go our separate ways."

"*Really* separate ways," Sam muttered.

"I can't wait," Jerry muttered back.

"Whoa!" Leroy said, caught in the middle between them. "How about we have ourselves a little truce here, okay? An agreement to keep personal matters until later, until after the business thing is done."

"Fine with me!" Sam said.

"Me too," Jerry seconded. "Let's just shut up and get this over with."

"*You* shut up," Sam told him.

"Don't tell me to shut up."

"I will if I want to!"

"I told you not to tell me to shut up, didn't I? The agreement, remember?"

"Oh, shut up," she taunted.

This bickering went on, back and forth, with Sam and Jerry ragging at each other as he drove them out into the desert. Jerry was starting to feel *very* tense, what with a hired killer beside him, and his ex-girlfriend nagging at him. He'd had enough, frankly.

"I swear to God, I'll crash this fucking truck right now!" Jerry threatened wildly.

"No, c'mon, don't do that," Leroy said.

"You hear me, Sam? I will! Say another word! One more word!" Jerry shouted at her.

Sam tried hard to resist, but this was a taunt, after all. Almost a challenge, really.

"Naugahyde!" she called out.

That did it. Jerry yanked the wheel hard to the right. The El Camino jumped over the shoulder, swerving wildly off the pavement into the desert, weaving through sagebrush and cactus, flying over small arroyos. On their present erratic course, they were barreling toward a telephone pole about a hundred feet ahead.

"You gonna shut up?" Jerry shouted.

"Jerry! Stop the car!" Sam yelled.

Jerry turned the wheel at the last second to avoid a collision. It was close. They fishtailed, brushing against the pole. And careened sideways, back toward the shoulder. A tire blew as they jumped over the shoulder back onto the pavement. The truck kept going, swerving out of control into the wrong lane, missing an oncoming truck by a heartbeat. At last they came to rest on the opposite side of the road.

Leroy let out a long breath he had been holding.

"Jerry," he said, "I want you to know, you're the craziest fucker I've ever met."

Twenty-two

The heat was like a furnace, merciless, shimmering in waves on the road. They were in the middle of nowhere. Just brown gravellike desert with scruffy sagebrush and distant mountains as far as the eye could see. Every five minutes or so a car zoomed by on the sunbaked pavement. It was about as desolate a spot to have a flat tire as you could ever hope to avoid.

Sam got out of the car on her side, slamming the door behind her.

"Go ahead!" Jerry shouted at her. "Go to Vegas!"

She gave Jerry a scathing look, then simply turned and walked away, momentarily out of words. Jerry watched Sam storm across the highway to the opposite shoulder and continue a little ways into the desert. As he watched her go, his anger deflated as completely as the flat tire he had caused. He knew he had fucked up. It didn't help that Leroy kept shaking his head, like he had seen gang wars and a lot of heavy shit come down, but *never* anything as savage as a man and woman in love.

Jerry got out of the El Camino and began foraging in the back for a tire and jack, leaving Leroy alone in the cab. As a professional, Leroy was fed up.

Sitting alone in the front seat, Leroy began to consider what he needed to do in order to get the basic agenda back on track here. He had been hired to deliver an antique pistol to Los Angeles. That was the beginning and end of his mission—very simple, only it hadn't turned out to be so easy after all. Leroy found himself staring at the closed glove compartment door, wondering if maybe Jerry had put the gun in there. It seemed way too easy, but then again, Jerry was an amateur, not a pro. After a while, just to satisfy his curiosity, Leroy tried to open the glove compartment door. But it was locked. In frustration, he slammed his fist into the compartment door, and it popped open. And there it was: the beautiful old pistol. He pulled it out of the glove compartment and examined it more closely. The gold and silver glittered in the sun. The gun was a lot heavier than it looked, very solidly made. Leroy had never held a weapon like this—a flintlock, from a time when people did not murder one another as efficiently as they did today. It was more than a weapon: it was a work of art. As an artist, of sorts, himself, Leroy appreciated the deadly beauty of the Mexican flintlock.

At last he replaced the pistol gently inside the glove compartment and shut the door. He reached inside his shirt pocket to check his plane ticket and the time of his flight out. Then he glanced at his watch. There was enough time for all the things that needed to be done, and catching his plane too. This job had been confusing for him, bringing up a bunch of emotions he would have preferred to leave alone. He had allowed himself to get off-track, and that was fatal for a man in his position. He knew what he had to do now. A smile touched the corners of his lips as he saw how easy it was. How beautiful, really, much like the old gun now in his possession.

Leroy slipped out of the passenger-side door and ambled around to the back of the vehicle, where Jerry was sitting with the spare tire on the ground next to him, trying to wrench the lug nuts free on the wheel that was flat. Leroy lit a cigarette and, inhaling lazily, watched Jerry work.

"For fuck's sake!" Jerry complained, working a stubborn lug nut with the star wrench.

"One time, I had a blowout in Florida," Leroy told him. "I mean, way the hell out, middle of nowhere. I get to the trunk—no spare. Four hours in the hot baking sun till some trucker came along. Now I always check."

Jerry was working too hard to answer. Two of the lug nuts were proving to be a problem, as they were completely frozen in place. Leroy glanced across the highway to where Sam was pacing back and forth a little ways off in the desert, talking to herself. The highway itself was momentarily clear of traffic.

This was the moment.

Leroy slowly pulled out his gun and pointed it at the back of Jerry's head. Jerry kept working, oblivious to the fact that he was about to die. Leroy looked up and down the highway one last time to make sure they were alone. But there was a problem now: a huge construction tractor truck convoy had just come around a bend from the north and was barreling down the road toward them followed by a line of other cars. This wouldn't do. Leroy tucked his gun back into his waistband.

"Lemme give it a rip," he offered, bending down. "Sometimes they need a little quick torque. Like, it's too much for the bastards to oil 'em once in a while."

Jerry stood up, allowing Leroy to take over the

dirty work. He watched the convoy of trucks thunder by as Leroy got to his knees and fitted the star wrench over one of the reluctant lug nuts. Leroy was about to give the wrench a serious yank when he caught a reflection of Jerry in the shiny hubcap. Jerry was standing over him with a gun in his hand pointed at Leroy's head. The curve of the hubcap distorted the proportions, but otherwise it made a perfect mirror. Leroy realized he had made a major mistake: if he could see Jerry, Jerry had been able to see him.

Leroy turned very slowly to face Jerry and the gun. He smiled a little, just to show there were no hard feelings. In his profession, someone won and someone lost. It was never personal. Leroy was still smiling when, fast as lightning, he went for his gun.

Sam was walking slowly, facing the mountains, when she heard the crack of gunfire. A single shot rent the desert air.

She turned in surprise. She ran back to the El Camino. She saw that Jerry was standing at the side of the vehicle with a gun held loosely in one hand, specks of blood on his shirt. Leroy was crumpled near the flat tire, obviously dead, his head a bloody mess.

"Walk away, baby. Walk away," Jerry told her.

Sam was hysterical. She screamed and began hitting Jerry repeatedly with all her might. He covered himself with his arms, but he was helpless against such an onslaught of fury.

"What the fuck did you do?" she screamed. "What did you do to Leroy?"

He tried his best to answer. "This guy was gonna kill us, right here! He wasn't gonna wait to get us to a destination! *Right here!*" he cried out.

He wasn't sure she even heard him. She was bawling, and ran over to Leroy's body.

"Wait a minute," Jerry suddenly said. "I *met* Leroy in 1997 in Minnesota . . . and that ain't him!"

"Jerry, you made a mistake. He was my friend!"

"Listen to me, Sam. Leroy is black! Okay? He was *black!*"

Sam stopped, gaping in astonishment. At this moment, she didn't seem to know which end was up, but what Jerry just said had finally gotten through to her, striking some responsive chord.

"No . . . ? No . . . ?" she managed.

"That's right, a person of color. African American."

Sam shook her head, scared and baffled. The strength seemed to evaporate out of her legs. She slumped down, staring lost into space.

"The guy at the hotel in Vegas was an African American," Sam said in quiet shock. "The guy he killed."

"Well, there you are! This is starting to make sense. Don't you see? *That* must have been Margolese's Leroy—the guy in Vegas. The *real* Leroy."

Sam didn't see. Frankly, she was beyond comprehending any of this. But Jerry was having himself a major revelatory moment. Suddenly a whole bunch of things were starting to make sense.

"And this guy . . . you know what? I am an asshole, a complete fucking asshole!" he cried, pacing up and down alongside the El Camino. He kept muttering to himself, like a madman. " 'This is your last chance, Jerry' . . . ha-fucking-ha! Something's going on all right! Sure, he talked to Nayman, of course, can't you see?"

Sam looked up from where she was sitting on the ground to where Jerry was pacing.

"What should I see?" she demanded.

"That something's going on," he told her.

She shook her head sadly. But Jerry was undeterred. Truth had yanked hold of him, a big lightning bolt of understanding had struck, and Jerry wasn't going to stop until he knew everything. He reached down and began rifling through the dead man's pockets, talking nonstop.

" 'Give the gun to fucking Leroy'? 'He'll get it on down to Margolese'? Bull-fucking-shit! *Bullshit!*"

Jerry pulled out the dead man's wallet, nodding to Sam fiendishly. "Nayman sent in this asshole to take out Leroy, get the gun, and hang it all on stupid fucking Jerry! Right?" He was tearing through the wallet, looking at the credit cards and driver's license. "Right! . . . Mr. Winston Baldry!"

"Winston?" Samantha managed, mouthing the name inaudibly, remembering the tattoo she had seen on the arm of the man she had known as Leroy.

"That's right! But I met Leroy, Mr. Baldry. I met him," Jerry cried at the dead man, triumphant. "And there's no way anybody could've known that, and that was your fucking mistake! I don't believe it! Oh, boy, every fucking chance I've ever had, I've blown it. But not this time, no. For once in my life, I win!"

Sam took the wallet from Jerry, and looked at the driver's license inside. Fresh tears spilled down her cheeks.

Jerry sank back against the hood of the truck, trying to catch his breath.

"I fucking won!" he celebrated. He pumped his fist in the air, nodding at Sam. "Oh my God. I'm lucky I didn't lose you three days ago," he said to her, more quietly.

Sam's eyes traveled from Jerry to where Leroy was crumpled dead on the ground by the flat tire. Only he wasn't Leroy anymore. He was some stranger named Winston Baldry.

"I want to go home," she sobbed.

Twenty-three

They drove in silence on the two-lane highway back toward the airport. The yellow lines streamed passed, spellbinding, hypnotic, mile after mile.

Jerry felt strangely peaceful, like he used to feel as a kid after a good long cry. But he was worried about Samantha and he kept glancing at her from time to time. She sat motionlessly, staring like a zombie out the window at the scenery whizzing by. He could see her eyes in the reflection of her window, red and swollen. He had no idea what she was thinking. He wished there was some way he could reach her, but he didn't know how. They were confined together in this car, a small tight universe, and they had never been further apart.

It was midafternoon by the time they arrived at Toluca Airport once again, where they had begun earlier in the morning. A full circle, except now there were two of them rather than three. Jerry was glad for Sam's sake that she was going home, back to her known world. He'd be home himself one of these days, if he ever got his passport again.

He parked, locked up the El Camino, and walked with her into the terminal, carrying her bag. Several times he started to say something to her, but his words dribbled away, useless.

Jerry and Samantha sat next to each other in silence on plastic bucket seats in the waiting area by Gate Six.

They had just called Sam's flight a second time. She stood up and looked at him, like she desperately wanted to say something. But she only sighed, shook her head, and turned to join the other passengers in line. Jerry watched as she gave a portion of her boarding pass to an attendant by the gate. Then she was gone, walking out from the terminal building into the bright sunlight and the jetliner that waited on the tarmac.

Jerry wandered to the big glass window where he could look out from the terminal to the tarmac below. He could see the back of Sam's head as she walked in line toward the brightly painted jet that waited a short distance away. The line got sluggish as it reached the metal stairs that had been wheeled up against the front of the plane. Sam glanced back at the terminal, to where he was standing at the window, but then very quickly she lowered her eyes to the ground. He wasn't certain if she had seen him or not. Probably not, he decided.

The line flowed slowly up the stairs. There was a tall man with a cowboy hat standing behind Sam, causing Jerry to occasionally lose sight of her.

Don't listen to the creep! he told her in his mind telepathically. He willed her to turn around and look back at him. To wave, at least, if nothing else. Show some sign that this wasn't the end forever. But all of Jerry's telepathy was to no avail: she didn't turn, she didn't wave. She was lost to him.

A fuel tanker drove by on the tarmac, between the boarding jetliner and the terminal, and he lost sight of her once more. When he could see the plane again, Samantha was really gone. Jerry felt sick to his stomach. He watched until everyone had boarded and they pulled the metal stairs away and closed the cabin door. He felt stunned, confused, and more hurt than he could ever remember feeling before.

He turned to leave and then, to his astonishment, there she was, standing in front of him.

"I want to ask you a question," she said. "It's a good one, so think about it."

He nodded as she put her bags down.

"If two people love each other, but they just can't seem to get it together, when do you get to that point of enough is enough?"

Jerry was overwhelmed. All he could see was Samantha standing there looking at him, obviously in a great deal of pain.

"Never!" he assured her quietly, his voice full of emotion.

Tears welled up in her eyes. And then, like magic, he was holding her in his arms.

Twenty-four

On their way back to the hotel, as Jerry drove past a crew of workmen fixing a stoplight, he reflected that love might be a many splendored thing, but it didn't solve all of his problems, not by a long shot. There was still the dangling question, for example, of how he was going to make amends with Big Boss Margolese and manage to stay alive long enough to live happily ever after with Sam.

These things required serious thought, and even before serious thought, he needed a passport. From the airport, Jerry drove himself and Sam to the Hotel Del Plaza, with Jerry explaining the whole story to Sam. The clerk seemed pleased to see him, welcoming him back like an old and valued friend. He even allowed Sam to phone the U.S. Consulate on the lobby phone, free of charge, while Jerry made himself as comfortable as he could on the authentic, beaten-wood lobby bench. It was a long afternoon, waiting for the bureaucratic wheels to move, and hopefully a return call. Mr. Williamson, who had been waiting for a such a call since March, was asleep at the far side of the lobby, snoring patiently.

"They'll call, Jerry," Sam assured him. "I've left sixty messages. I said it was an emergency."

Five minutes later, hearkening back to all that Jerry had told her in the car, Sam asked: "Why would Nayman ask you if you like sex and travel? What's that supposed to mean? What, does he think you fool around or something?"

Jerry's mouth fell open in surprise.

"After I told you this whole long debacle, *this* you have a problem with?"

"Well, I think asking someone who's involved in a relationship of the heart if he likes sex and travel—it's mean-spirited. It's stupid. And I'll tell you this—we're not running anymore. We're through running. Sooner or later, that phone's gonna ring, we'll get your passport in order, and you can place that gun in Margolese's hand, where it belongs."

Jerry nodded, trying to maintain an optimistic attitude. But knowing Big Boss Margolese, he wasn't so sure he could.

"Nayman is fucking Margolese—that's got nothing to do with us," Sam assured him, sensing his doubt. "Jerry, by some grace of God, or I don't know what, you've managed to Forrest Gump our way through this. If we run now, we'll be running our whole lives."

She paused significantly and said, "Jerry, we want our life back."

He thought over what she said. "Yeah, baby, we do," he agreed. But unlike Sam, he knew it would take a miracle.

Ten minutes later, the desk clerk walked over. What the desk clerk said wasn't a major miracle, perhaps, but it *was* a ray of hope:

"Señor Welbach, Mr. Ted is calling."

Jerry put the receiver to his ear and listened. Very gradually, a huge smile came to his face.

"Well?" Sam asked, when he put down the phone.

"You'll never believe it!" he assured her.

The fiesta to celebrate the coming marriage was held that night at the house of Joe, the owner of the pawnshop. Jerry and Sam followed the directions that Ted had given them, winding up and down narrow dirt lanes. They would have gotten lost several times except for the mariachi music that guided them, distant at first, but growing louder the closer they got.

Joe lived in a rambling two-story house of peeling stucco walls, with a backyard where long tables had been set up for all the guests. Colored lights had been strung out among the trees overhead and the mariachi band was really going wild, trumpets and guitars blaring and people singing at the top of their voices. Ted was in the middle of all the gaiety, surrounded by about sixty-five members of his newly acquired extended family, doing a traditional dance with Emmanuelle, with a huge grin on his face.

Jerry stood next to Sam, hardly believing his eyes. Ted was really moving and he looked ten years younger than the last time Jerry had seen him. Jerry and Sam got pulled into the dancing—there was no way to avoid all the friendly hands urging them to join in the celebration. Jerry didn't quite know the right moves, but he managed a kind of salsa disco. Sam matched his steps, adding a little flamenco rock 'n' roll, grinning at him, her eyes glittering in the reflection of the colored lights overhead, happier than he had seen her in a long time.

It was a magical night; there was joy in the air. And then there was the food. After the dancing, Jerry and Sam were led to a place of honor at one of the long outside tables, where they were waited on hand and foot, and served plate after plate of incredible traditional foods, tastier than any Mexican cuisine Jerry had ever eaten in California. There were enchiladas, tacos, salsa, avocado to die for picked ripe from the trees, chilies rellenos, some pork dish in a mole sauce, fresh shrimp with lime and cilantro. Plus lots and lots of ice-cold Mexican beer—tequila too, though Jerry avoided the hard stuff tonight in deference to Sam, trying to show her what a brand-new domesticated guy he could be.

Soon after they arrived, Ted had greeted Sam and Jerry with huge, happy hugs, but being the center of the celebration, Ted did not have a chance to really speak with Jerry for several hours. After dinner, he gestured for Jerry to join him inside the house, leaving Samantha and Emmanuelle together at the long table to become acquainted. Ted led the way inside a large, old-fashioned kitchen that was crowded with about ten women, all of them busy stirring pots, opening ovens, and organizing the next wave of food that was to be brought outside. Personally, Jerry couldn't imagine eating another bite more. One of the women stopped to squeeze Ted's cheeks as she walked outside with a tray.

"That's old Joe's wife," Ted told Jerry. "This is the

best thing that ever happened to me, Jerry, the best. I want the same happiness for you."

"I'm glad for you, Ted. I really am. Hey, look, you got my passport?"

"You bet."

They switched passports and Jerry felt just a little further along on the great treadmill of life: for the time being, he had his girl, the pistol, his passport, his rental car—he was even well-fed.

Ted was nodding at him. "You want some free advice? You're not getting out of here tonight. Last flight was an hour ago. I'm telling you, listen to Sam—get on the line with Margolese in jail, first thing, and tell him about Nayman giving him the screw job."

"I don't know," Jerry sighed. "You think it'd do any good?"

Ted put his arm around Jerry's shoulder. "He was your way into this life, Jerry. You know he's your only way out. . . . Look at that!" Ted said softly, smiling through the open door at Sam and Emmanuelle. He sighed with domesticated satisfaction.

"You'll always be my guy, Jerry!"

Twenty-five

Jerry and Sam slept late the following morning, later than he had intended, waking in each other's arms in a creaky double bed at the Hotel Del Plaza.

Jerry's mouth was dry but his body was happy with remembered music, good food, and the long, slow rhythms of a more personal kind of dancing Jerry and Sam had performed until nearly dawn, after they had made their way back to the hotel after Ted's party.

He took a shower and came back into the bedroom to find Sam watching a Mexican soap opera on TV. Jerry picked up the phone on the bedside table and called the number of the California prison where Big Boss Margolese had been incarcerated the last five years, due to the fact that his Caddy had been rear-ended and his trunk had popped open, courtesy of Jerry Welbach.

Jerry wasn't certain he was hearing the prison operator correctly.

"No, that must be wrong," he said. "Could you please check it again? . . . Please. Margolese. M as in Mary . . . Can you turn that down?" he said to Sam. "You don't even speak Spanish, honey."

"Real emotion transcends language," she assured him. "You don't have to understand the words to hear their pain, Jerry."

Jerry frowned as the prison operator came back on the line. "Well, that's impossible," he said into the receiver. "Do you know when? . . . No, thank you."

Jerry hung up the phone with a puzzled expression. Sam looked at him, waiting for the news.

"Margolese is out of jail," he told her. "He got released this morning. He's *out*. What's going on here? He's not supposed to be out until Thursday."

Sam raised an eyebrow. "It *is* Thursday, Jerry."

Jerry was absorbing this news when he heard the brown junkyard dog barking wildly from outside. It was a bark Jerry had come to recognize well, though he had never heard the dog quite so excited as this. Frankly, he had been hoping the dog had found a new home. Jerry pulled back the window curtain to see what was happening outside.

"What's going on?" Sam asked.

"I dunno."

Peering out of their second-floor window, Jerry could see over the railing of the outside walkway to the parking lot below. The ugly brown dog was sitting next to the El Camino, barking his head off. But there was nobody in the parking lot anywhere near the car, nothing going on outside at all. Just an empty, locked-up car and a dog going crazy. It was very puzzling.

Jerry was alarmed. His vacation from hell south of the border had taught him that anything that could go wrong *did* go wrong in this country. Very quickly, he rummaged through his luggage for the jinxed antique pistol. He was looking about the room wildly, trying to think of a good hiding place, when Sam held out her hand.

"Gimme it," she said, taking the pistol.

He couldn't imagine what she had in mind. She took out a scarf and lifted her dress, showing a whole lot of lovely leg, one of Sam's nicest features. Jerry was starting to think she had something kinky in mind, but in fact her plan was very simple: she tightened the scarf around her leg like a garter, stuck the barrel of the pistol into the material, and when she lowered her dress again, the gun was fairly well hidden, as long as she was standing up and not bending too much the wrong way.

Jerry slipped out of the door to the outside walkway, holding his .38 revolver loosely at his side, all his senses alert for danger. Down below, the brown dog was still barking at the El Camino without any apparent reason. Jerry hurried along the walkway to the flight of stairs outside that went down to the parking lot. He approached his rental car cautiously. When he was about ten feet away from the El Camino, the dog suddenly cowered and ran off across the lot, looking scared, his scruffy tail between his old legs. Jerry raised the gun and tiptoed the last few feet to the car. He peered through the windshield and couldn't believe his eyes. There was a man inside curled up on the front seat, fast asleep.

This was some nerve! Jerry raised his .38 and angrily tapped the barrel against the glass in order to get the individual's attention. But the man didn't even stir. If it weren't for the fact that Jerry could see a rhythmic heaving of breath, he would have worried the guy was dead. Drunk was more likely the situation.

"Hey!" he called, knocking a second time on the glass.

But the guy just lay there, snoozing away without a care. Jerry tried the door, but it was locked from the inside and Jerry had stupidly left the keys upstairs in the room.

He pounded on the glass again, angrily. But the man on the front seat did not move.

While Jerry was trying to figure out the mystery of why some person had appropriated his rental car for a bedroom, another man was stalking silently down the second-floor walkway toward Jerry and Samantha's room, keeping his eye on the parking lot below, hoping that Jerry wouldn't turn around. The man was an expert at opening hotel doors, but in this instance, his professional skills were not required: the gringo had left his door unlocked, unwisely. The man slipped inside noiselessly, closing the door behind him.

He stood very quietly inside the doorway, looking and listening hard. The hotel room appeared to be empty, but he had learned never to take anything for granted. The bed was messed up, in a tangle of sheets. The TV was on softly to a Mexican soap opera. This surprised the man because he had been told the gringo didn't speak Spanish.

The Mexican man walked soundlessly into the bathroom to find that there was nobody there also. He looked behind the shower curtain, then went back to the bedroom to check inside the closet. But again, there was no one. With time running out, and no need now to be so quiet, he began pulling clothes out from the closet onto the floor. There were two open canvas bags near the dressing table, full of personal belongings, and he dumped the contents onto the unmade bed. Next he went through the drawers, tearing the room apart. But he did not find what he was after.

There was not time for a truly thorough search. The man looked at his watch, shook his head with disappointment, and crept out of the room as silently as he had entered, closing the door behind him with a soft click.

If the man had been inside the hotel room a few minutes later, he would have been surprised to see the bed begin to wiggle, most mysteriously. A hand came out from between the mattress and the boxspring, and a moment later, a woman's head. Samantha Barzel, somewhat squashed and scared, crawled out from her hiding spot and hurried to the door, bolting the security lock and closing the little chain. She knew very well that one good kick from a relatively strong man and the door would fly open. Still, the locks gave her a small feeling of security.

She wondered how Jerry was doing in the parking lot.

*   *   *

Jerry was still standing in bewilderment alongside his rental car, pounding at the glass, trying to rouse the sleeping man on the front seat.

From Jerry's perspective, a number of things seemed to happen at once. First, he heard a loud whistle behind him. He spun around and saw a man looking down at him from the walkway railing outside his and Sam's room. The whistle appeared to be a signal. Jerry sensed movement from inside the car. He spun back around and saw that the man who was asleep was now opening his eyes and sitting up.

He felt a tap on his shoulder, and this time when he spun around, he saw two men standing directly behind him. One of the men was huge, a real gorilla. The other was slight and short, and he was smiling at Jerry in an almost tender manner. Jerry had seen him before. It was the thief who had stolen his El Camino, and whose foot Jerry had shot in the desert.

Jerry was taking in these facts, the reappearance of an individual he had hoped never to see again, when the gorilla by the thief's side raised his fist and proceeded to smash Jerry in the face.

Jerry's lights went out.

Twenty-six

Jerry awoke slowly, experiencing various stages of pain. First, there was light, an all-pervasive glare shining down on him. Then there was heat, thirst, and a blinding headache.

He heard men's voices nearby, speaking in Spanish, laughing roughly among themselves. Jerry was lying on the hard ground, his mouth in the dust. After a long while, he found the courage to open his eyes. He was somewhere out in the desert in an old wooden barn.

Jerry saw the thief who had stolen his El Camino approach him, his right foot in a cast.

"Gringo!" the thief called. "You've been out so long, your clothes are out of style!"

Jerry felt awful. His face was raw and swollen. He could only see out of one eye. There was a taste of blood in his mouth and his nose felt somehow loose, not entirely attached to his head. He watched anxiously as the thief hobbled closer with the use of a cane. He used the cane to tap Jerry on the shoulder.

"How's the trip coming along, my American friend? Good?" he asked.

"I'm enjoying it. *Viva Mexico*, man!" Jerry managed. "No hard feelings?"

"I'm Mexican, lucky for you. We're very forgiving people, maybe too much so. Add to that, I'm Catholic."

There were three men near the thief, and they all crossed themselves at the mention of their religion.

"He got you on the beak there, eh?" the thief asked, looking at Jerry's nose with some concern.

Jerry touched it and winced. "Yeah, I think it's broken."

"Oh, sure it is. Sure." He said something in Spanish to the other *banditos*. Jerry recognized the word *agua* and hoped they were really going to bring him some water. "The mistake, America, was thinking I didn't know what the pistol was," the thief continued in English. "It's a tale told to all children of Mexico. Did you sell it?"

Jerry didn't answer.

The thief nodded to the big guy, the gorilla who had put Jerry's lights out earlier. The gorilla shot his hand out and gripped Jerry's nose, hard enough to cause Jerry to scream.

"No! For fuck's sake! *No!*" Jerry answered in pain.

"That's good," the thief told him, handing Jerry a canteen of water. "Very good. It's cursed, that gun."

The thief drove the old pickup truck that Jerry had traded his wristwatch for, what seemed like a few lifetimes ago. Jerry had left the truck behind at the cantina when he had repossessed his rented El Camino. Frankly, he was amazed the shitbox Ford still ran, but thieves and machines seemed to amble along in a different, more amiable universe here in Mexico than up north.

Jerry had no idea where they were going. The thief's gang of *banditos* had dragged him into the passenger seat and then they piled into the back. The thief himself was behind the wheel, ignoring the difficulties of managing the clutch, gas pedal, and brakes with his right foot in a cast. The old truck sputtered along in jerky starts and stops down the dirt road through the empty desert.

He bounced along, half dreaming, as the thief told him the story of the old gun.

The day was upon him. Today the gunsmith would present his gift to the nobleman and his son. The sun seared the arid town square as every villager lined up along the dirt road, expectantly awaiting the nobleman's arrival.

The gunsmith and his beautiful daughter—he in his Sunday best and she wearing a shimmering white wedding gown and veil—waited patiently by a small wood podium adorned with decorations. The young assistant also waited nearby. On top of the podium rested an ornately carved wooden box, inside which lay the antique pistol. The gunsmith fussed over the box, making sure it was positioned just right on the podium so that when it was opened the gun would catch the sun's bright light and make for the perfect presentation.

Suddenly, a small boy yelled down to the town square from above, announcing that the nobleman was fast approaching. Everyone scrambled to get ready to greet him as a flock of bridesmaids fussed over the reluctant bride-to-be. The gunsmith stood ramrod straight at attention as a hush fell over the crowd.

The nobleman and his son rounded a corner and came into view, the son astride a great white stallion. The nobleman's son was a cruel and horrible-looking young man, with a crude scar running down his face. He was a notoriously vicious soldier, worldly and wicked. Twenty dusty soldiers followed on horseback, filing into position behind the nobleman and his son.

The nobleman and his terrible son cantered up to the podium and looked down on the gunsmith, who bowed and lowered his head deferentially as he offered his daughter to them. The daughter stood waiting in her flowing gown in silence, locking eyes with the nobleman's son, glaring at him through her veil in pure hatred. The son nodded his head in approval, clearly impressed with the young woman's beauty. The son turned to face his father with an eager, filthy grin twisting on his face.

The assistant held their mounts as they lowered themselves off of their steeds and walked over to the trembling gunsmith. They all shook hands as the nobleman introduced his son; then he turned toward the box on the podium.

The nobleman was expecting something more beautiful, more perfect than he'd ever laid eyes on before. As the gunsmith presented the box to the nobleman, he held it appreciatively before slowly lifting the lid. His eyes were blinded by the light that emanated from the box. Nothing—no words or description—could have given justice to it or prepared them for the gun's flawless grace. They were stunned.

The nobleman picked up the gun and held it aloft, twisting it in the fiery sunlight. It was, indeed, the most beautiful weapon anyone had ever seen. Loud cheers rose up into the air.

The young assistant looked over to his love, the gunsmith's daughter, and he returned her loving gaze. As her *veil drifted in the breeze, his heart ached—he had never seen her look as beautiful as she did right at that moment. But just then, the nobleman's son walked up slowly to the waiting bride and raised her veil to reveal her lovely face, now set in stone. When the nobleman's son saw his intended bride-to-be, it was love at first sight. He bent to kiss her softly on the lips, but the gunsmith's daughter did not respond. Rather she fought to control her revulsion and conjure the strength to remain standing during this violation.*

Not seeing her abhorrence, the crowd sighed at the sight. But the nobleman's son did as he stared into her saddened eyes, knowing in his cruel heart that he would make her learn to love him. Ecstatic, the gunsmith snapped his fingers. The gathered throng separated to reveal a clay pitcher resting on top of the barrel. The nobleman beckoned to his son, then handed him the pistol. The nobleman's son took the mighty weapon in his hands—it was a perfect fit.

The assistant looked on, every moment an eternity. He was lost in love's gaze, his eyes locked on the scene before him. The soldiers and the townspeople stood back as the son inspected the weapon, then carefully leveled the pistol to his target. Steadying the gun, he squeezed the trigger.

Click!

Nothing happened, not even a fizzle. The nobleman cut his eyes to the gunsmith, who immediately turned beet red and shrugged his shoulders. The gun did not work: the curse had rendered it useless in unworthy hands. The assistant, noting this, nodded slightly to himself, a smile creeping to his eyes.

The nobleman took it as a bad omen, but the gunsmith urged him to try it one last time. And so he did. As the townsfolk grumbled, the gunsmith walked over took the pistol, and examined it. Then he handed it back to the nobleman's son. Once again, he pointed it at the clay pitcher and squeezed the trigger. And once again, nothing happened.

The townsfolk began to giggle and laugh as the nobleman grew insulted by the ineptness of the poor gunsmith. The gunsmith begged for the nobleman's understanding and tried his best to placate him. As they argued, the assistant nodded clandestinely to the bride, who was so overcome by joy she could only smile through her tears, trembling with happiness.

The nobleman's son caught the daughter's overjoyed smile, but mistaking it for mirth at his expense, he saw that her gaze extended beyond him. He turned to see who she was looking at, realizing that she was sharing the moment with the young assistant, who was decidedly younger, stronger, and more handsome than he.

When the nobleman's son realized that her heart belonged to the poor simple assistant—a man far less than he in stature and wealth—he was furious. His heart burned with envy and rejection as he turned to face her. She nodded slightly to let the nobleman's son know that, indeed, his suspicions were correct.

Suddenly, the nobleman's son drew his service revolver from his holster and pointed it at the assistant, not being able to bear the humiliation. The bride screamed as every eye in the square turned to the tense situation that was unfolding. She picked up the gunsmith's pistol and pointed it squarely at the nobleman's son. The soldiers responded immediately by cocking their own guns at the bride, who held her ground.

The gunsmith was horrified. The nobleman watched the grave scene, not believing his eyes. Silence descended on the square as the nobleman's son defiantly dared the bride to fire the incompetent pistol, laughing as he tightened his own grip around his revolver.

The assistant, realizing that even if the gun should work she would certainly die, begged his love to withdraw and accept their fate. His handsome face calmly reassured her, and she complied, lowering the gun to her side, surrendering. The nobleman's son also nodded, accepting victory, then quickly pivoted toward the assistant and fired three times, killing him.

Some say that you could actually hear her heart break. Unable to scream, enveloped in the sudden, terrible fi-

nality, and confused by the nobleman's son's ruthlessness, the bride beckoned for him to draw near. As the nobleman's son began to walk toward her, she abruptly pressed the barrel of the beautiful pistol to her temple and pulled the trigger.

Bang!

With that one motion, she fearlessly surrendered her bitter spirit to purgatory. The entire square was stunned, but none more than the nobleman's son, who was amazed at the undaunted manner with which she ended her own life for love. The bride's dress fluttered in the stifling breeze as the ornate pistol rested in the sand where it fell.

Twenty-seven

When he had finished the tale, the thief fell silent as he continued to drive the truck down a dusty desert road, God only knew where. Jerry sighed. Despite his broken nose, and the fact that he felt like roadkill, the bittersweet tragedy of the legend got to him.

"The pistol contains her damned soul," the thief said after a while. "It's not your fault you know nothing about this gun. You're America. This gun does not belong to you."

The thief shook his head with a fatalism that worried Jerry. They continued driving far into the remote desert. At last they came to a drift driveway that led to a peaceful compound where children played noisily outside. Wherever they were, this appeared to be the end of the line. The huge gorilla *bandito* jumped out from the back of the truck and took Jerry by the arm, pulling him roughly from the cab. The thief walked around from the driver's seat and together they led Jerry toward the house.

The thief smiled knowingly. He opened the front door and gently pushed Jerry inside. After being in the bright sunlight, it took Jerry's good eye—the one that wasn't swollen shut—a few moments to adapt to the darkness. The interior was small but surprisingly well furnished, with two wingback chairs occupied by two forms. As Jerry's eyes adjusted, he could see that there was a very old man, shrunken and wrinkled, sitting in a chair gazing at him curiously. Jerry stared back, trying to read his fate in the old man's eyes. But the old man revealed nothing. Jerry then turned to look at the person sitting next to the old man, and he nearly had a heart attack.

It was Big Boss Arnold Margolese himself. He looked smaller than when Jerry had last seen him. Jerry was so shocked he wasn't able to speak immediately. Finally he cleared his throat and stuttered, "Mr. Margolese, I don't understand."

The Big Boss shook his head sadly. "What's it's going to take, Jerry?"

Jerry could only gape in bewilderment.

"Take for what?" he asked.

"For the gun, Jerry," the Big Boss explained.

"What's it gonna take for you to give it to me, and not to another?"

Jerry was hurt and stunned that the Big Boss thought he might be betraying him.

"Man!" Jerry exclaimed in disbelief. "I don't know what it's gonna take. I'm new in the fuck-you business. You tell me—what does it take?"

Margolese continued to study Jerry, almost abstractly. Like Jerry was a creature from another planet that needed to be dissected and examined.

"Jerry," he explained. "I never fucked you. I had Nayman send you down here. I didn't know he was looking for a buyer." The Big Boss gestured to the thief and his associates, who had come into the house behind Jerry. "They told me he was looking for a buyer, and I didn't know who from my team was still *on* my team. Or even if there still *was* a goddamn team."

"And who the fuck are these guys?" Jerry asked, looking around at the *banditos*.

"They work for this man, Tropillo," he answered, nodding at the old man seated next to him.

"Well, who's he?" Jerry asked. But suddenly he saw how convoluted this whole deal was, and realized he didn't even want to know. "You know, that's not even important. You give me one good reason why I shouldn't fight to my death to *not* give you the gun. And believe me, if it comes to that, someone here'll walk away from it missing an ear, or not being able to fuck anymore, I'll tell you that . . . *one* reason! Now that you let me know what you think I'm made of!"

After Jerry's outburst, it was so quiet in the house, you could hear a pin drop. People generally did not speak to Big Boss Margolese in this manner.

Margolese didn't answer right away. "Are you a fatalist, Jerry?" he asked finally, rising and approaching Jerry.

"I never really thought about it."

"Well, when you think about the afternoon you smashed into my life, into my car, you ever think there's anything to that?"

Jerry shrugged. Philosophy had never been a huge part of his daily life. "I honestly never even thought about it," he admitted.

The Big Boss lowered his voice and leaned forward intently in his chair. "Because of that afternoon, I'm doomed to remember the backward inmate with a paper clipping. When you're in jail, a small box, you get to learn a lot about the fella you're in the cage with."

Jerry saw that Margolese was holding a photograph in his hand, offering it to Jerry. The quality was not good. It showed a thin young Mexican man standing in the jail yard with Margolese, who was wrinkling his face up into the harsh light of the sun. Jerry studied the photograph, not certain what he was supposed to make of it. After all, it was just two men in a prison yard. He handed it back to the Big Boss.

"I grew to love him, like he was my own son, Jerry. But he was his," Margolese said, gesturing to Tropillo. "The boy came to me one day with a paper clipping. 'This is my destiny, this is my birthright,' he said to me. It was a story about the pistol. How they found it in a mine, stashed away. He slept with that clipping, he ate with it, all day long he just looked at it. Every day, he'd tell me that when he got out he would find it and return it to his father, whose father's father had crafted the gun."

Jerry looked at Tropillo with new interest. Feeling the closeness of the legend so near at hand, it gave Jerry goose bumps. The old man nodded again, his tired eyes smiling.

"Eighteen months later, he took it in the belly for me," Margolese was saying, speaking about Tropillo's son. "He died. I vowed to search and acquire the pistol, and return it to his father. My grandson

Beck was a headstrong boy, sure. He was mixed up. He didn't understand the honor behind what I was doing. It became clear to me that I had to send you down, because you were the instrument in the situation, Jerry. His son is dead, my grandson is dead—all of it brought together by that afternoon at our intersection."

The Big Boss paused meaningfully, staring hard at Jerry, who sat down overwhelmed. Jerry was taken aback by Margolese's belief in that destiny, all set in motion by Jerry running that red light at Ventura Boulevard. A karmic collision. Any minute, they might start reading Tarot cards or tea leaves, Jerry thought to himself. It wasn't what he would have expected for an old gangster, but if there was one thing he'd learned on this crazy adventure, it was that human nature was a puzzlement. Despite himself, he couldn't help but be a little moved.

"That's a pretty fucking good reason," Jerry agreed.

The old man, Tropillo, had been studying Jerry with intense interest the whole time. He said something in Spanish and one of his men translated.

Jerry walked closer. Tropillo was so old and shriveled, but still elegant and stately.

"He said, 'You are a foot soldier of God.' "

Jerry liked how that sounded. It elevated all the sleazy bullshit he'd been experiencing recently to heroic proportions. The old man pointed to a place on the wall behind him, a special spot where there were two crosses and some photos. But the middle was empty.

The old man kept talking. "She's safe there—right there, she'll be safe, and she can fly with angels. No devil can catch her here. Right here, she can fly with angels."

Now, literally speaking, what the thief had just translated did not make a great deal of coherent sense. Standing here with a broken nose in this house in the desert, in front of a wrinkled old man with knowing eyes, Jerry saw the light. The empty nook was where the beautiful old pistol belonged, so it could fly with angels. And he, Jerry Welbach, was instrumental in the plan, tapped by fate to rear-end a gangster's Cadillac so that all these events might come to pass. It really couldn't be any simpler.

Jerry turned from the old man back to Big Boss Margolese and nodded.

"Are we square?" he asked.

"I'll owe you," said the gangster.

Twenty-eight

Back at their room at the Hotel Del Plaza, Samantha was pacing back and forth, worried sick about Jerry. Suddenly the phone rang, scaring her half to death. At first she wasn't sure if she wanted to pick it up or not. Too many bad things had happened recently, and she wasn't certain she could take anything more. But maybe it was Jerry. She reached for the receiver and clutched it to her ear.

"Jerry? *Honey?* Hello?"

There was a pause; then a strange man spoke.

"I bet this is the Queen of the Idiots—am I right? This must be Sam?"

Sam didn't answer. She was spooked by the unfamiliar voice, uncertain, under the circumstances, whether it was wise to admit anything, much less her identity.

"This is Bernie Nayman," the voice went on. "Where's that stupid fucking Jerry and Ted? Are they with Leroy?"

This made Sam angry; nobody had the right to say "stupid fucking Jerry" except herself.

"Don't you mean Winston?" she asked archly. "I hope not, 'cause Winston is dead."

Nayman was silent. Sam could hear him breathing and thinking hard on the other end.

"Then you're in a lot of trouble," he said finally, "especially if Jerry sold that gun."

"Jerry hid the gun."

"A step in the right direction," Nayman told her. "Are you there, Sam?"

"Yeah, I'm here."

"Yeah, me too," he announced.

Just then, Nayman appeared in the doorway.

Twenty-nine

Bernie Nayman leaned against the trunk of his rented Grand Marquis outside the Hotel Del Plaza, waiting in the hot sun. He had left the car door open, with the radio on, playing an old American pop song that had been translated into Spanish. Bernie Nayman didn't like Mexico very much. Personally, he couldn't wait to get this business over with so he could get back to L.A., a city where people cared about the important things of life: money and getting ahead.

All in all, he didn't think that he was going to have to wait too much longer. Like always, Nayman had the winning hand. The song on the radio was just ending when he saw a shitty old Ford pickup truck sputtering and farting down the road, coming in his direction. Jerry Welbach was behind the wheel. There were three Mexican guys in the back, and another

Mexican in the passenger seat next to Jerry. But they weren't going to be able to help Jerry too much, not with Nayman holding all the cards. It was a tense situation.

Nayman smiled, enjoying himself. Life was good when you were a shark swimming in a pool with guppies. The pickup truck came to a stop in a cloud of dust a few feet from where Nayman's Grand Marquis was parked. The engine coughed and died and the three Mexicans in the back of the truck jumped out and immediately pointed their guns at him. Nayman raised his own revolver, which he had been holding loosely at his side, the hammer cocked. With his other hand, he raised his palm, telling them to stop.

Jerry and the thief got out from the cab of the truck. The thief said something in Spanish to his three *banditos*, and they began to spread out along the pavement.

"Tell them to stop walking, or you're dead, amigo," Nayman said calmly, aiming directly at the thief. "This thing spits lead."

The thief said something quickly to his men, and they complied.

"Where is she?" Jerry asked dangerously. "What did you do?"

Nayman grinned and patted the truck. He loved how Jerry's face turned sickly white. In addition to his pallid complexion, it looked as if someone had really beaten the crapola out of him.

"If she's in the trunk, dead . . . " Jerry began, but he was too upset even to complete his threat.

"Well, it *is* hot in there," Nayman agreed.

"Let her out!"

Nayman nodded and got to the point. "Give me the gun, I'll let her out. That's the deal."

"Where're the keys, Nayman?" Jerry demanded.

Nayman looked suitably vague, patting his pocket with his free hand. "Jeez!" he said. "I might have lost them."

"Then you're shit out of luck," Jerry told him. " 'Cause only she knows where the pistol is."

Nayman studied Jerry's face to see if Jerry was shitting him. He didn't think so. Jerry was too stupid to lie well, Nayman thought; his face told the entire story of what was going on inside his loser's brain.

"Well, let's ask her then," Nayman said with a smile, taking the car key from his pocket and opening the trunk.

Sam sat up in the trunk of the car, holding the beautiful old pistol, pointing it directly at Bernie Nayman, who shifted his own gun to point first at

Jerry, then at Sam, then at Jerry again. The three *banditos* stepped back out of the way at the sight of the gun, leaving Jerry, the thief, Bernie Nayman, and Samantha in an interesting predicament that was ironically similar to the predicament that happened long ago, between the nobleman, the nobleman's son, the gunsmith, the handsome young man who was his assistant, and the gunsmith's beautiful daughter.

Nayman laughed. "Put that down," he told her. "You'll damage it."

"I'll use it!" Sam threatened.

Jerry shook his head, trying to get her attention, as did the thief and his three *banditos*. Apparently Sam didn't quite understand the uncertain nature of the weapon she held in her hand.

"Sam do not—I repeat, do *not* pull that trigger, baby," Jerry urged. "No, no, no . . ."

"I'll pull the trigger! I will!" she promised. Her hands were shaking, making the barrel of the gun waver back and forth wildly.

Very calmly, Nayman raised his own gun and pointed it at Jerry.

"Toast that gun, he's dead right after," Nayman assured her.

The stand-off was complete. Jerry looked at Sam and nodded very gently for her to put the gun down.

His face was curiously calm and handsome at the moment, despite his broken nose, reassuring her that everything would be fine. *If she would only put the gun down!*

As for Sam, she stared at Jerry. Their eyes were locked together. Her finger was still on the trigger, but this was a big decision she needed to make and she seemed uncertain what to do.

She turned to Bernie Nayman.

"Do you like sex and travel?" she asked him.

"As a matter of fact, I do," he answered.

"Wrong answer!"

Sam squeezed the trigger.

Boom!

The noise was terrible and it looked to those who were watching as though the tip of the gun barrel had exploded, sending forth a bullet as well as something round and shiny. Bernie Nayman stood there gurgling, shot in the throat. His eyes grew wide and he just stood there for a long moment—before finally crumpling to the ground.

"We just witnessed a miracle!" the thief said, stunned.

In fact, they were all stunned: Jerry, the thief, the *banditos*, and Sam, who dropped the pistol and slid out of the trunk of the car onto to the ground, astonished at what she had done. The Mexicans crossed themselves, unable to take their eyes from the cursed pistol that had fallen on the sandy gravel of the parking lot.

The thief was the first to move. He walked to the pistol and picked it up, reverently. The tip of the barrel had blown clear off, but the rest of the gun was intact, the sunlight reflecting against its polished gold and silver. As the thief held the old weapon, enraptured by its dangerous beauty, Jerry walked closer to where Bernie Nayman was lying dead, and began searching around on the ground near his body. After a moment, he saw the piece of gold that had flown off the gun when it had fired, now glittering on the gravel, lying next to a bent piece of gun casing. He reached down to retrieve the gold. It was a golden O, a perfect ring that had been ejected from the barrel when it had exploded.

Jerry held the golden ring up to the sunlight, studying it closely. He then looked up to the thief, holding his eyes and nodding as if asking, "Can I keep this?"

The thief nodded gravely. "It would be our honor."

Jerry walked to where Sam was sitting on the ground, leaning against a wall. He kneeled down next to her and very gently slipped the golden ring from the gun down upon the fourth finger of her left hand.

Amazingly—one might almost say miraculously— it was a perfect fit. As they kissed, the Mexicans started up their truck and began to drive off. The mangy dog turned away from Jerry and Sam and ran after the truck, jumping in the back as it rolled off toward the Mexican horizon.

Thirty

The elegant old man, Tropillo, was smiling to himself. He looked down at the mangy dog by his side. He was overjoyed to see the old pistol back in its special nook, flying with the angels . . . just as Jerry and Sam were themselves flying down the open highway in the El Camino toward the airport, with many angels fluttering in their hearts.

"Do you love me, Jerry?" Samantha asked, snuggling next to him as the highway flowed by, spellbinding. She held the gold ring on her finger up to the afternoon light.

"You know I do, sweetheart," he told her.

"Then, tell me it again."

"I already told you three times, honey."

"I just want to hear it again."

The El Camino roared through a crossroads, the

desert heat shimmering like a mirage on the pavement. Above the intersection, a light turned green, yellow, and red, over and over again, just like Jerry's dream.

He stroked her hair, his arm around her shoulder as he drove. She closed her eyes and listened to Jerry relate the old tale once again.

The pistol was crafted for a nobleman by a poor Mexican gunsmith. He fashioned the gun as a gift to go along with the hopes that the nobleman's son would take his only daughter's hand in marriage. . . .

She could see it so clearly: the dusty town plaza, the handsome young man, and the beautiful girl. All of it mixed together now with her own life and Jerry's, somehow golden, transformed by the legend of the Mexican gun.